EVA

Peter Dickinson was born in Africa, within earshot of the Victoria Falls. When he was seven, his family moved to England, where he later graduated from Cambridge. For seventeen years he worked on the staff of the magazine *Punch* before starting his career as a writer – which he knew he was meant for since he was five years old. His first book was published in 1968, and since then he has written more than fifty novels for adults and young readers. In 1999 he was one of three writers chosen for the short-list for Britain's first Children's Laureate, and in 2000 he was shortlisted for the International Hans Christian Andersen Award.

Among his award-winning children's books are *City of Gold* (Carnegie Medal), *Tulku* (Carnegie Medal and Whitbread Children's Book of the Year), *AK* (Whitbread Children's Book of the Year Award) and *The Blue Hawk* (Guardian Children's Fiction Award). *Eva* was highly commended for the Carnegie Medal.

Praise for *Eva*:

'Shatteringly moving, readable.'
Junior Bookshelf

'It is highly provocative, it has tenderness, humour and passion. It involves the reader from the very first page and will not quickly leave the mind.'
Times Literary Supplement

EVA

Peter Dickinson

MACMILLAN CHILDREN'S BOOKS

First published in Great Britain 1988 by Victor Gollancz Ltd

This edition published 2001 by Macmillan Children's Books
a division of Pan Macmillan Ltd
20 New Wharf Road, London N1 9RR
Basingstoke and Oxford
www.panmacmillan.com

Associated companies throughout the world

ISBN 0 330 48384 6

5 7 9 8 6

A CIP catalogue record for this book is available from
the British Library.

Typeset by Intype London Ltd
Printed and bound in Great Britain by Mackays of Chatham plc, Kent

PART ONE
WAKING

DAY ONE

Waking . . .
Strange . . .
Dream about trees? Oh, come back! Come . . .
Lost . . .
But so strange . . .

Eva was lying on her back. That was strange enough.
She always slept face down. Now she only knew that
she wasn't by the sensation of upness and downness
– she couldn't actually feel the pressure of the mattress against her back. She couldn't feel anything. She
couldn't be floating? Still dreaming?

 . . . tried to feel with a hand if the mattress

 . . . Stuck!

nightmare. Mum's voice.
and the shape was Mum's face. She could see the blue
eyes and the mouth now.

She tried to smile but her lips wouldn't move.
'It's all right, darling. You're going to be all right.'
There was something terrible in the voice.

'Do you know me, darling? Can you understand what I'm saying? Close your eyes and open them again.'

The lids moved slow as syrup. When she opened them she could see better, Mum's face almost clear, but still just blur beyond.

'Oh, darling!'

Relief and joy in the voice now, but something else still, underneath.

'You're going to be all right, darling. Don't worry. You've been unconscious for . . . for a long time. Now you're going to start getting better. You aren't really paralysed. You can't move anything except your eyes yet, but you will soon, bit by bit, until you're running about again, good as new.'

Eva closed her eyes. A picnic? Yes, on the seashore – Dad standing at the wave-edge holding Grunt's hand on one side and Bobo's on the other, all three shapes almost black against the glitter off the ripples. And after that? Nothing.

'Is she asleep?' whispered Mum.

As Eva opened her eyes she heard a faint electronic mutter, and this time she could see clearly enough to notice a thing like a hearing aid tucked in under the black coil of hair by Mum's left ear.

'I don't know if you can remember the accident, darling. We're all right too, Dad and me, just a bit bruised. Grunt broke his wrist – the chimps got loose in the car, you see – on the way back from the seaside. Can you remember? One blink for yes and two for no, all right?'

Eva opened and closed the heavy lids, twice.

'Oh, darling, it's so wonderful to have you back!

I've only got five minutes, because I mustn't wear you out, and then they'll put you back to sleep for a while. Look, this is a toy they've made for you, until you're really better.'

She held up a small black keyboard.

'They're going to start letting you move your left hand in a day or two,' she said. 'If everything goes well, I mean. So you can use this to do things for yourself, like switching the shaper off and on. What's the code for that?'

She'd asked the question to the air. The mutter answered. She pressed a few keys and a zone hummed, out of sight at the foot of the bed. At the same time a mirror in the ceiling directly above Eva's head began to move, showing her first a patch of carpet and then the corner of some kind of machine that stood close by the foot of the bed and then the zone as it sprang to life. It must have been a news programme or something, an immense crowd stretching _____ wide street, banners, the drifting trails

_____
up . . .'

Eva had closed her eyes to answer yes but the lids didn't seem to want to open. She heard the slats of the blind rattle up, and a slight whine directly overhead as the mirror tilted to show her the window.

'Oh, darling,' said Mum's voice, further away now.

There was something in it – had been all along, in spite of the happiness in the words. A difficulty, a sense of effort . . .

A door opened and closed. For a while Eva lay with her eyes shut, expecting to drift off to sleep, back into the dream, but stopped by the need to try and puzzle out what Mum had told her. There'd been an accident in the car on the way back from the picnic, caused by the chimps getting loose. Grunt probably – he was always up to something. She'd been unconscious since then, and now she was lying here, in some kind of hospital probably, unable to move. But it was going to be all right. They were going to let her start moving her left hand in a day or two, and then later on the rest of her, bit by bit . . .

Really? Mum wouldn't have lied – she never did. If it had been Dad, now . . .

Her forehead tried to frown but wouldn't move. She'd heard of people being paralysed after accidents, and then bits of them getting better, but the doctors *letting* it happen . . .?

And the keyboard and the mirror – that showed it was going to take a long time, or they wouldn't have bothered . . .

Something was dragging her down towards darkness. She willed herself awake. She fought to open her eyes. They wouldn't. But almost . . .

A reason to open them . . . something to see . . . the window, Mum had said. She must look out of the window, see . . .

Suckingly the lids heaved up. A blur of bright light, clearing, clearing, and now a white ceiling with a large mirror tilted to show the window. The light dazzled. After the long darkness it was almost like pain, but Eva forced herself to stare through it, waiting for her eyes to adapt to the glare. Now there was mist still, but it was in the mirror. An enormous sky, pale, pale blue. Light streaming sideways beneath it, glittering into diamonds where it struck the windows of the nearer towers. Tower beyond tower, far into the distance, all rising out of mist, the familiar, slightly brownish floating dawn mist that you always seemed to get in the city at the start of a fine day. She must be a long way up in a tower herself, she could see so far. Later on, as the city's half-billion inhabitants began to stir about their streets the mist would rise, thinning as it rose, becoming just a haze but stopping you seeing more than the first few dozen towers. But now under the clear dawn sky in the sideways light of a winter sunrise Eva could see eighty, ninety miles, halfway perhaps to the further shore where the city ended. She felt a sudden surge of hap-

blond beard, greying slightly, sat watching a shaper-zone which showed the scene Eva's mother had just left, the small figure on the white hospital bed ringed by its attendant machines and lit by the sunrise beyond the window. A younger man and woman in lab coats sat at computer consoles with a battery of

VDUS in front of them, and an older woman in a thick, stained jersey and lopsided skirt stood at their shoulders watching the displays.

Eva's mother settled herself onto the arm of the first man's chair and put her hand into his.

'Well done,' he whispered.

There was silence for a minute.

'She doesn't want to go to sleep,' said the man at the console. 'Trying to get her eyes open.'

'Let her,' said the older woman.

The shape in the zone raised its eyelids. Clear brown eyes stared up. Slowly the wide pupils contracted.

'She knew me,' said Eva's mother. 'At least she knew me.'

The older woman turned at her voice and came over to stand beside her, looking down at the zone.

'Yes, she certainly knew you, Mrs Adamson,' she said. 'You were the first thing she saw and recognized. That was essential. Now she is seeing a familiar view. That can do nothing but good.'

'If only she could smile or something. If only I could feel she was happy.'

'I cannot let her use her face-muscles for a long while yet. She must not attempt to speak until most of her main bodily functions are firmly reimplanted. But for happiness . . . Ginny! A microshot of endorphin. And then put her back to sleep.'

Eva's mother started to sob. The older woman patted clumsily at her shoulder.

'Don't cry, Mrs Adamson,' she said. 'It's going to be all right. We've brought it off, in spite of everything. Your daughter's all there.'

8

She turned and went back to the control area. The man rose and followed her. They stood watching the displays and talking in low voices. But Eva's mother sat motionless, staring at the zone, searching for a signal, the hint of a message, while beyond the imaged window the image of sunrise brightened into the image of day.

DAY SIX

Waking again . . .
Still strange . . .
Stranger each time, more certainly strange . . .
But surely the dream had been there, unchanged. The
* trees . . .*
Lost . . .
Loster than ever . . .

Already Eva had got into a waking habit. She would
keep her eyes shut and try to remember something
about the dream, and fail. Then she would feel with
her left hand for the keyboard and check that she'd
left the mirror angled towards the window, and that
nobody had come in and changed it while she'd been
asleep. And then, still with her eyes shut, she'd guess
what time of day or night it was – they let her stay
awake for more than an hour now, and then put her
back to sleep for a while and woke her up again, so it
might be any time – and what the weather was. And
last of all she'd open her eyes and see if she'd guessed
right.

First, what time? Not where were the hands on the
clock, but where was the sun? Up *there*. It didn't seem
like guessing. She could sense the presence of the sun,
almost like a pressure, a weight, despite the layers of
tower above her. The weather, though? She didn't feel

so sure about that, but it had been sunny the last few wakings, so a fine day, late morning . . .

She opened her eyes.

Spot on. The sun up *there*. She could tell by the stretching shadows under the sills of the tower of the University Library. The city haze was more than halfway up the nearer towers, and as it thickened with distance it seemed to rise higher, so that only the tops of the further towers showed here and there, like rocks in a sea, and beyond that they vanished altogether. Nice guess, Eva – only it wasn't a guess. Funny how sure she felt about the sun. She couldn't remember that happening before the accident.

Next she practised using the keyboard. Mum had called it a toy, but if so it was an extremely expensive one. A very clever gadget indeed. It lay strapped in place beneath her hand, and the keys were so arranged that she could just reach all of them. It didn't only do the things Mum had said, like moving the mirror and switching the shaper off and on and

It spoke not with a dry electronic voice, but with a human voice, Eva's real voice, taken from old home-shaper discs and sorted into all its possible sounds and stored in a memory to be used any way she wanted. It was tricky, like learning to play the violin or something. Practice wasn't just getting her hand to know the keys and then work faster and faster; it was also putting in a sentence and then getting the voice to say it different ways ('Mary *had* a little lamb!' '*Mary* had a little lamb?' 'Mary had a leetle lamb.').

Dad said it had been specially built for her by scientists in the Communications Faculty. His blue eyes, paler and harder than Mum's, had sparkled with excitement while he showed her its tricks – it was just his sort of toy. Eva, to be honest, had been less excited – OK, the boffins were friends of Dad's – the Chimp Pool was technically part of the University, and this room was in the Medical Faculty – and they'd been amused to see what they could do. Even so it must mean, surely, that nobody expected her to start speaking properly for a long time – months. Years? Ever? But Mum had said . . .

No she hadn't. She'd talked about running around, not about speaking.

The thought came and went as Eva practised, until suddenly she got irritated with her slowness and switched the shaper on instead. A thriller of some sort – a woman desperately pushing her way in the wrong direction along a crowded traveller – not that. A flivver-rally, the sky patterned with bright machines, the buzz of thousands of rotors – not that. A beach, kilometres of shore-line invisible under human bodies, the white surf bobbing with human heads – not that. People, people, people. Ah, trees . . .

Only a cartoon, actually, one she used to watch a lot when she was smaller, because of the heroine's name. It was called 'Adam and Eve' and the plot was always the same. Adam and Eve were the first people and they were king and queen of the jungle. Adam ruled the animals and Eve ruled the plants. Their enemy was the Great Snake. Adam and Eve were trying to drive him out of their jungle so that it would be safe for them to have children, but Adam was always getting into trouble – usually a trap set by the Great Snake – because of his arrogance and impulsiveness, and then Eve had to get him out of it by her plant magic. It was rather wishy-washy, but pretty to look at. All round the world hundreds of millions of little girls waited in ecstasy for the moment when Eve would begin her plant-magic. Dad said the company spent huge amounts on research to make sure they put in what little girls wanted.

Now Eva watched, pleased by the greenness and the shapes of leaf and branch. Eve was following a trail through the jungle. Adam was in a mess somewhere, no doubt. The plants moved twigs and tendrils to show Eve the way he'd gone. She came to a cave mouth. She put a seed in the earth and caused a flower to spring up, a single white cup like a shaper-

now this morning. She never used

didn't feel like practising with her voice again, so for something to do she told the mirror to go back and show her the view. She watched the reflections as it swung to its new position, mostly carpet and the corners of things: a bit of trolley, one of the machines that monitored and fed her and took her waste away, the air-conditioner, the window. The forest of towers, the millions of people, people, people . . .

The crammed streets, the crammed beaches, the crammed skies, they were only a fraction of them. Most people stayed in their rooms all day, just to get away from each other. A lot of them never went out at all. Their world was four walls, and their shaper-zone. Dad said that the shaper companies were the real rulers of the world. The people told them what they wanted and the companies gave it to them and nothing else mattered. The view from the window was beautiful, until you thought about the people.

Eva lost patience again and told the mirror to go somewhere else. The only place it knew was the visitor's chair. She watched as it swung – the air-conditioner, the machine, the trolley, the blank zone, another machine, the chair . . .

The long way round – it could have gone straight across the bed . . .

Why . . .?

They didn't want her to see the bed!

That note in Mum's voice, the effort, the sorrow. The keyboard, the trouble they'd taken. The way they'd set the mirror. The accident. You can get very badly smashed in an accident.

'What a pretty baby!' strangers used to say. 'What a lovely little girl!' Later, just looks and smiles that said the same – glances and stares from boys when she came into a new class. She'd had Mum's oval face but Dad's high cheekbones, eyes a darker blue than either of them, long black gleaming hair, straight nose, full mouth . . . She'd moved like a dancer, easily, fallen without thought into graceful poses . . .

No!

But she had to know, to see. Urgently she moved the mirror again, back to the window. It swung the whole way round, of course. She tried confusing it, stopping it, giving it fresh instructions before it had finished a movement. No good . . .

The door opened and shut, and Mum was standing by the bed. She was pale. Her mass of hair was a mess, with a lot of grey showing in the glossy black. There were hard lines down beside her nostrils. She looked as though she hadn't slept for a year. Her smile wasn't real.

'Hello, my darling,' she whispered. 'I'm sorry I'm late. How are you today?'

She bent and kissed Eva on her numb forehead. A strand of her hair trailed across Eva's face. It didn't tickle, because the face was numb too, but Eva automatically closed that eye to let it pass. Mum turned

hand under the bedclothes to grasp Eva's

'What are you doing, you funny girl?'

Eva answered the cool grip with a squeeze, but she could feel Mum's jumpiness, and hear the false note in the lightness she tried to put into her voice. Her hand was wrong too. Too small. Deep in the nightmare now Eva stared up into Mum's questioning eyes. They were wrong too, something different about the colour. She forced herself to close one eye again, and then the other, squinting inwards as she did so.

Her nose was gone.

Most of the time you don't see your nose at all, but if you shut one eye and look sideways there it is, that fuzzy hummock, too close to focus. It was gone. At the lower rim of vision she could see the vague blur of a cheek and at the top the darker fringe of an eyebrow, much more noticeable – much more *there* – than it used to be . . .

Mum wasn't even pretending to smile now.

Eva closed both eyes and willed the nightmare into day. The accident. Her whole face must have got so badly smashed that they couldn't rebuild it, or not yet, anyway. They were keeping it numb so that it didn't hurt. Her jaw and mouth must be so bad that she wouldn't be able to speak properly for ages – never perhaps – so they'd made her her voice-box instead. They didn't want her to see herself in the mirror . . .

She wriggled her fingers out of Mum's grip and slowly found the right keys. No point in fussing with tones. She pressed the 'Speak' bar.

'Let me see,' said her voice, dead flat.

'Darling . . .' croaked Mum.

A whisper rustled in the speaker by her ear. She stopped to listen. Eva pressed out another message.

'Let me see. Or I'll go mad. Wondering.'

'She's right,' said Mum to the air. 'No, it's too late . . . No.'

16

The murmur started again. Eva gripped Mum's hand again and closed her eyes. Why was the hand so small? Had her own hand . . . The thumb was all wrong! Why hadn't she noticed? It was . . .

Without her touching the keys the mirror-motor whined. She kept her eyes closed until it stopped.

'I love you, darling,' said Mum. 'I love you.'

Eva willed her eyes to open.

For an instant all she seemed to see was nightmare. Mess. A giant spider-web, broken and tangled on the pillows with the furry black body of the spider dead in the middle of it. And then the mess made sense.

She closed her right eye and watched the brown left eye in the mirror close as she did so. The web – it wasn't broken – was tubes and sensor-wires connecting the machines around the bed to the pink-and-black thing in the centre. She stared. Her mind wouldn't work. She couldn't think, only feel – feel Mum's tension, Mum's grief, as much as her own ＿＿＿＿＿. Poor Mum – her lovely blue-eyed daugh-

name. Then it came. Carefully ＿＿＿＿＿

She used the tone control to sound cheerful.

'Hi, Kelly,' said her voice.

Kelly was – had been – a young female chimpanzee.

*

17

Eva had grown up with chimps.

As more and more people crammed into the world, needing more and more land for cities and crops, so the animals had died out. Most of the great wild jungles were gone, and the savannahs that used to cover half a continent. Here and there a few patches of jungle remained among mountains too steep to use, or stretches of bleak and barren upland unsuitable for the energy fields that filled most of the old hot deserts, or offshore waters where fish-farms for some reason wouldn't flourish, but even these were always being nibbled away as somebody found a new method of exploiting them. And anyway, the wild animals that had been crowded into those pockets had destroyed them by their numbers, or become diseased, or just somehow lost interest in living in a world like that.

The big animals vanished first, elephants and giraffes, gorillas and orangs, whales and dolphins. Others hung on in the patches and crannies people left for them, by mistake or on purpose. A few actually thrived because living in a world full of people suited them in ways they could adapt to – there were no eagles any more, but you could see kestrels any day in the city, nesting among the towers or hovering in the updraughts between them, living off mice and sparrows and other small creatures which in turn lived off the scraps that people littered around. There were rats, of course, and wasps, and city pigeons and starlings, and so on, but that was all.

There'd been zoos for a while, but what was the point of going to see a few sad old elephants in an enclosure when you could go to a shaper-park and walk among the shapes of an elephant herd, life-size, wallowing in the shape of a mud-pool while the shape of a lion stalked the shape of an eland beyond (all stored on old tapes, made before the last savannahs had gone)? And at home there were wild-life programmes on the shaper, either old tapes or live from the little patches of jungle and desert that still were left. You could have them in your living room, hear their screams and songs, watch their hunting and mating. They weren't life-size, of course, and you couldn't smell them, and when they killed and ate each other the blood disappeared from your carpet as soon as you switched channels. Besides, a real rhinoceros, living the life it was made for, needs a dozen square kilometres. A taped rhinoceros only needs a few cubic centimetres. So it was all very tidy and sensible, just right for a world crammed full of people. That's what people had thought, until it was too late. And that is why there were only the chimps left.

were different. Chimps were a special case,
lose to humans, our cousins
chimps alive, for

weren't really
ested in real chimps. More
almost. Easily the most popular ads on
were for a soft drink called Honeybear which used live chimps, dressed up as people. All the cities had branches of the International Chimp Pool where you

could go and see a few chimps in big cages. But the main sections of the Pool were right here, part of the University, and Eva's Dad was Director of Primate Zoology, in charge of research. So Eva had grown up among chimps.

In fact she'd been one of Dad's Research Projects. Of course she'd met humans her own age, because Mum and Dad like other parents put their child into playgroups so that she would learn to socialize, but Eva had always felt just as at home among chimps. In some ways more, in fact – she'd been making chimp-chatter before she said her first human word, and before she was three Dad had been using her to help him understand how the chimps' minds were working. He knew almost everything there was to know about them, from the outside, but Eva could joke with their jokes, feel with their feelings, see why some simple-to-humans problem baffled them when they could solve trickier-looking problems almost at once.

Of course Mum and Dad had needed to be careful. A small chimp is enormously stronger than a human baby; it's even cleverer for the first few months; but Eva had soon learnt how to behave, how to use the grunts and gestures which meant 'You're the boss', and 'Please', and 'Sorry, didn't mean it', and so on. She'd got along with chimps pretty well, always.

And now she was one herself. OK.

She felt a sort of mild amazement. All her feelings were calm, a bit dreamy. They must be pumping something into her bloodstream, she reckoned, to control her shock and rejection. This must be real panic-time for them out there, whoever they were who whispered into the little speaker in Mum's ear. Anyway, there were questions to ask. She pressed keys.

'How . . .?'

No need to say any more with Mum. With Dad you'd have had to spell the question right out, but Mum was used to hints and garblings because she worked in the Housing Bureau, helping ordinary people sort out ordinary problems like rent-arrears or rowdy neighbours or trying to get away with an unlicensed pregnancy.

'It's something called neurone memory, darling,' said Mum. 'Dad says you'll have learnt about it at school, so you probably know more than me. You were in an irreversible coma after the accident, and Joan Pradesh heard about it and said she'd try and . . . and do *this*, if we wanted. She's never done a human before, you see. It was a risk, she said, but we thought, in the end . . . well . . . your poor body, it was so broken, and just lying there . . . anyway we said yes. ~~And it's~~ worked. That's marvellous, isn't it? But now ~~. . . patient~~ and just lie and wait for ~~. . . another.~~

course. And yes, ~~. . .~~ The thing is, you aren't just a lot of ~~. . .~~ ecules bundled together inside a skin – you're that too, but that's not what makes you *you*. What *you* are is a pattern, an arrangement, different from any other pattern that ever was, or will be. Your pattern

21

began to grow from the moment you were conceived, but the bits that make you so sure you are *you* came later; your discoveries of the world, from your first blurred peerings with your baby eyes, and all your thoughts and imaginings and dreams and memories make up that pattern, and are kept there by the neurones in your brain which have sent their wriggling axons branching and joining and passing messages to each other through the incredible complex networks they have grown into. What old Professor Pradesh, Joan's father, had found was that the pattern actually 'remembers' how it got there, and given the right treatment and an 'empty' brain it can be persuaded to go through the whole process over again. Professor Pradesh had made his discovery with very simple creatures, flat-worms mainly, but Joan had carried the research on until she was working with mammals, all the way up to chimps. And now, humans.

Eva pressed a few keys.

'How long?' said her voice.

'Two hundred and thirty-eight days.'

It was the wrong answer, for once. Even so, Eva's mind juddered with the thought. Eight whole months gone from your life, blank! Of course it would take that long for the pattern to grow – in the first Eva it had taken almost fourteen years.

'No,' she said. 'How long till?'

'Sorry,' said Mum. 'It was just . . .'

Of course. She knew the exact count of days. She'd felt each of them grind through her, never knowing if the risk would be worth it, or if she'd get no more than part of her daughter back, or perhaps just a mumbling kind of nobody trapped in Kelly's body. No wonder she looked so much older. The speaker-whisper stopped. Mum nodded.

'Joan's been saying you mustn't try and start waking muscles up before they're ready. You must try not even to think about it. Just let it happen. She wasn't really ready for you to find out what . . . what's happened, but now you *have* found out she's probably going to change her plans and start letting you move your face-muscles. She didn't want to before because you'd have tried to talk . . .'

The whisper started again. Eva lay looking at the face in the mirror. Me, she thought. Not Kelly, me. Goodbye, blue eyes, goodbye soft pale skin, goodbye nose. Perhaps Kelly had been pretty – pretty to another chimp. Except that chimps didn't seem to think like that, judging by the way the males used to go mad about moth-eaten old Rosie when she was in season . . .

The brown eyes peered down in the way you might ~~~~ animal. Was there a glimmer there? Eva,

~~~~ ready to

shadows.

'Sleep now, please,' said her voice.

They let her go gently. Her last thought was to wonder what had happened to Kelly, the real Kelly, the one who used to live in this furry skin. Where was *she* now?

DAY SEVEN

Waking again . . .
The dream . . .
Keep it. Hold on. Hold on . . .
Waking.

Perhaps they'd let her wake gently, so that the dream
had floated up with her almost to the surface, or perhaps it was just the idea of holding, because that
was one of the things in the dream, but at any rate
Eva woke and found that this time she could really
remember what she'd been dreaming. It was still
very strange, not like any of the dreams she usually
had. There was no story, no adventures, only the
idea, the images, the feelings – herself, moving
among branches, reaching with long arms, swinging,
holding . . .

Holding with her feet if she chose.

She lay with her eyes shut, living the dream again.
Then, instead of angling the mirror to show her the
window, left it where it had been when they sent her
to sleep. She opened her eyes and looked.

The blind was up and morning light streamed
across the bed. The face in the mirror, surrounded by
its tangle of tubes and cables, was still that of a
stranger. Large pale ears stuck out either side through
strong black hair; in the middle was the pinky-brown

hummock of the face-parts, with the huge lips, the nothing nose and the forward-facing nostrils; the brown eyes were bright with thought. She pressed keys. Deliberately she filled her mind with ideas of welcome.

'Hi, there,' said her voice.

Was there a glimmer in the eyes? Kelly's answer? Or just the reflection of Eva's own signal? No knowing.

'You've never seen a tree,' she said.

That mightn't be quite true. The chimps in the Research Section of the Pool had metal and plastic frames to climb on, but Dad always took a couple on family outings if he could, so Kelly might have seen trees in the city parks, but she'd certainly not have been allowed to climb one because of the difficulty of getting her down and the damage she might do while she was up there. In any case those would have been city trees, tamed, guarded, numbered, precious. The trees in the dream had been wild, part of a forest no

lion people living and working together, beginning form between the towers. She could still see about five miles. Nothing. The city stretched on far beyond that, far beyond sight on the clearest morning, endless. Like the forest in the dream.

Of course, Eva thought, I might have put the dream

25

there. Me. Eva. Knowing when I went to sleep that I was living in a chimp's body, I might have put chimp arms and feet into the dream. I might have invented the forest, from things I've seen on shaper pro-grammes. Only . . .

Only I was having the dream before I knew about Kelly. And it was the same dream. Perhaps knowing just helped me think about it, hold on to it, but it was there before any of that. Perhaps it isn't my dream at all – not Eva's, I mean. Perhaps it's Kelly's.

Hi, Kelly. You there?

The mirror was angled to show the window, so she sent the unspoken message inwards. She wasn't real-ly serious. It was more of a private joke, a whimsy. Her lips twitched. She actually felt them move.

Oh, great, she thought. They're letting me have my mouth back. She moved the mirror to show her the bed again and tried a smile. The image above her wrinkled its mouth at the corners.

There was a game you could play with small chimps before they became too strong for you to hold still. You put the chimp on your lap, gripping its arms to stop it grabbing, and then you moved a grape across in front of its face and watched a sort of wave ripple along the lips from side to side, following the grape, trying to suck it in. Chimps use their long and mobile mouths almost like an extra hand, for feeling and touching and trying things out, as well as all the grimaces that make up a lot of chimp-language.

Forgetting about the dream Eva lay and experi-mented. There wasn't a lot she could try, because they didn't seem to have woken her other face-muscles yet, or her jaw, but it was exciting enough to be able to

move anything at all. She hadn't really begun before
Dad came in.

'Hi, kid,' he said.

'Sorry,' she tapped. 'Fun.'

A slight pause while he put in the missing words.
You didn't get this sort of blip with Mum, but Dad
thought in proper sentences, with verbs and so on.

'That's fine,' he said. 'Only don't push it – we'll
have to see how it all goes. How are you feeling?'

'Funny. Things in my blood?'

He didn't get it.

'Stop shock?' she added.

The pause was different this time, while he decided
how much to tell her.

'Well, yes,' he said. 'We felt it was safer. As Mum
told you, your neurone linkages appear complete, but
we have no way of knowing how secure they are. You
have been through an extremely risky procedure, my
darling. We calculated that there were about four
        in five that we would fail.'

wonder whether

Dad shook his head as if he was trying
picture out of his mind.

'You have to remember that with you we are in
new territory,' he said. 'You are the first of Joan's sub-
jects to be capable of influencing the procedure of

neurone memory by conscious thought. You are the first to be properly aware of the passage of time, and therefore to be able to wish to hurry the process along. You are also the first to whom we have felt the kind of moral responsibility one has towards a human being. All this means that we are going to—'

'Hey!'

Eva had found how to make her toy do a sort of squawk which she used as a 'Hey!' code. Conversations were boring if you couldn't interrupt, but it still took a second or two to work. Dad stopped, blinked, thought back.

'Of course we have a moral responsibility to all living things,' he said. 'As a zoologist, life is my trade, so I feel this more strongly than most. I feel it especially towards chimpanzees. Still, it is different from the responsibility we have towards any single human being. OK?'

Eva would have liked to argue, but it would have taken too long, and anyway Dad was difficult to argue with, and her own thoughts were all in a mess, so she said nothing. Dad, typically, assumed she'd agreed.

'Now, the danger-point does not lie in your conscious mind,' he said. 'You understand and can accept that what we've done was, as you said, the only hope. The danger lies at the unconscious level, over which you don't have the same control. That is why we have to control it for you, for the time being, until it too has learnt to accept what has happened. It is the danger point for two reasons – first, as I say, because you can't persuade it by rational means not to reject your new body, and second because it is itself the main interface with that body. When you think, you think with a human mind. When you blink, you blink with a chimpanzee's involuntary reaction. Your own subconscious mind lies along that border. It is not of course as simple as that but that will have to do. The upshot is that we are going to have to be very cautious indeed about reducing any drugs which help suppress your subconscious tendency to rejection.'

'OK. Only little as poss.'

'You will have to cooperate with Mrs Alonso, who will be your psychiatrist. Her main preoccupation in the next few weeks will be to watch out for the slightest signs that . . .'

Eva switched off. She couldn't help it. She'd only been awake about twenty minutes but she felt exhausted already. What Dad was telling her was vital, and she should have been straining to understand every detail, but the way he did it made her mind go numb. It used to do that sometimes, even before. Dad was a natural explainer, lecturer, _____ facts into orderly patterns. _____ and

Now it drifted _____ Mum and Dad and Eva, having supp_____ ordinary day, Dad talking, Mum listening, and Eva looking out of the window and watching a million lights come on as dusk thickened across the city. Suppers must have been sad this last year, she thought. Not all families loved each other. Eva had friends one of whose parents had left, or perhaps both had stayed, but they'd bitched and quarrelled.

She'd been luckier than some. She'd felt pretty secure, always. But suppose something – she couldn't think what – had happened which had forced her parents to choose between their jobs and their family, well, there wouldn't have been any question with Mum; Mum was interested in her work and thought it was worth doing, but she wouldn't have hesitated. With Dad, you couldn't be sure. If he'd had to give up his work he'd have given up half himself. More than half, perhaps. So perhaps he wouldn't . . .

She looked at him as he leaned over the bed, explaining. Just beyond his head the mirror showed a bald patch in the middle of his scalp. It fascinated her. She longed to be able to sit up and rootle among the browny-grey hairs. From beyond the reflected scalp her own face gazed down. Seeing the man's head and the chimp's so close together she was struck by a thought.

'Hey!'

Dad stopped and waited, a bit impatient.

'Kelly's brain?' said Eva. 'Big enough?'

'Yes. You have in fact got about 120 cc less than you used to have, but luckily there is a bit of waste space in brains. I think you'll find you're all there, darling. Where was I? Oh, yes . . .'

But Eva had stopped listening again. The thought of grapes had returned, not out of her conscious mind but up from below. A whole bunch of grapes, purple, the bloom untouched, the skins bulging with sweet juices. Saliva spurted inside her mouth and a machine

30

sucked it away. She could actually feel it happening, which meant they were letting her have more of her mouth back. How long since she'd really eaten, how long since she'd had a taste on her tongue? Not since that picnic at the sea.

Dad had cocked his head to listen to the metallic whisper in his ear.

'Right,' he said. 'Apparently you're due for a nap, darling. Take it easy. Don't try to hurry things up, and you'll do fine. See you tomorrow, eh?'

Already Eva could feel the drift to darkness. She pressed a few keys.

'Love to Mum.'

'Yes, of course.'

Her eyes had closed before he was through the door. The first thing I'll ask for is grapes, she thought. Kelly would have loved grapes. All chimps do.

DAY SEVENTEEN

Waking . . .
Leaving the trees, the green shadows, the leaf-light . . .
Leaving the dream . . .

But the dream itself was changing. It was Eva's fault.
Sometimes even in the middle of the dream she was
aware of herself as a human mind, an alien in the forest. She had thought about the dream, knowing
everything the human Eva knew, so now as she
reached and clambered and rested she carried the
human knowledge with her.

The simplest change was that sometimes the
dreams had stories. These might be a plus. She had
adventures. She might look down between the
branches and see men, wearing clothes and carrying
guns, walking on the forest floor, and she'd know the
way you do in dreams that they had time-travelled
from the future and were coming to cut down the forest so that a city could be built which would house
the overflow of people from the bursting future
world, and only Eva could stop them. Sometimes the
stories were a minus. In the worst of these she was
digging into a termite nest and found just below the
surface a human face, Eva's own old face, gazing with
blank blue eyes at the sky, still alive, but with ants
going in and out of the nostrils. Mostly the dreams

were neither plus nor minus but muddled, the way human dreams are. The one she called Kelly's dream hadn't been like that. It had been simple, until Eva had brought her knowledge into it. She would never have it like that again.

She dreamed ordinary human dreams too, doing and seeing things in her old body, but nearly always the one she woke with was the one about trees. Then she would lie with her eyes shut and decide where she wanted the mirror, what would be the first thing she saw. Though she always chose the same it was still a conscious decision, an effort of will not to go back to the old game of guessing the weather. She opened her eyes and gazed up and made her voice say 'Hi.' As soon as they gave her her jaw and throat back she added the proper little pant and grimace of greeting, and tried to mean it. That helped.

Dad had been right. Suppose she'd woken and seen what they'd done to her and her bloodstream hadn't ~~been stuffed~~ with dope to help her stand the shock, ~~what used to be Eva, would~~

she told Mrs Alonso ~~
~~her so much – they put the dope right back up ~~ started again, but Eva knew she couldn't live like that for ever. Kelly's body wasn't just something she had to get used to, it was something she had to learn to be happy about. OK, it *was* better than dying, but that

wasn't enough. You had to wake and open your eyes and see your new face and like what you saw. You had to make the human greeting and the chimp greeting and mean them.

The old Eva could never have done it, the one who used to skate and ski and play netball for Lower School. They'd been right to make her come to life slowly, bit by bit, rejoicing in having a mouth to chew with, a throat that would swallow, a real moving arm she could lift and look at. Every day, as a sort of exercise, she forced herself to think of the third Eva, the one who'd come in between, after the accident but before the waking, a sort of nothing person, a sleeping mind in a smashed body. It was *that* that she had to compare this new Eva with, not the girl who used to skate and ski. This must be better than that.

Sometimes when they removed a tube or a wire the place where it had joined felt sore, and even that was a plus. To be hurt, you have to be alive.

Alive, but clumsy. The first movements, lip-ripples and hoots and chewings, had been misleading. The morning they let her have her arm back she woke and realized that in her last minutes of sleep she had been caressing her hand along her hairy thigh, troubled in her dream because the fingers could feel and the thigh couldn't, so it was like stroking a rug. Then she was awake and found her whole arm moving. She had made her greetings to the face in the mirror before she realized what had happened. Gingerly she pulled the arm out and held it up with the palm half open, and saw the arm and hand in the mirror stretch down towards her in the gesture chimps make when they

34

are asking for help or comfort. She stared at the glossy blue-black hairs then drew the arm down and lip-nibbled comfortingly along it, thinking, 'So this is me now. Me. Not Kelly up in the mirror. Me down here. OK.'

When breakfast came she tried to feed herself, putting the food into her mouth. She managed it by shutting her eyes and feeling for the next morsel. From then on the hand knew the way to the mouth. But when she tried to guide the hand by looking in the mirror she kept going the wrong way and missing, sometimes by inches. This didn't bother her much. Being able to move the arm at all was thrilling. But later that morning she found it wasn't just the confusion of trying to do things in a mirror which had been spoiling her aim.

They must have decided to give her a nap – they could still do that. Then they woke her up and she opened her eyes to see a stranger smiling down at her, a gorgeous young man with gleaming level teeth and

been such an effort and her voice had come out slow and stupid that she'd settled for chimp-grunts. You could say quite a bit with those.)

'OK, OK,' said Robbo. 'We're not shipping you off to colonize Vega Three. That's what I trained for, teaching ordinary folk like you and me . . .'

(He said it without a flicker. He was clever as well as pretty.)

'. . . how to use their bodies when they're upside. Trouble is, there's not so much of that happening just now, so my firm have loaned me across to try and give you a hand. Right?'

He bent out of sight, but watching in the mirror Eva saw him jointing some steel rods together into a structure which turned out, when he rose and stood it by the bed, to be a framework suspending a cord above her chest. He clipped a blue ball to the end of the cord.

'Let's see you touch that without moving it,' he said.

Eva lifted her arm and stretched it out. Her fingers bumped into the ball a good couple of inches before she expected. She clicked irritation.

'Oh, not that bad,' said Robbo. 'Give it another go.'

He steadied the ball and she tried again. And again and again. By concentrating hard she learnt to touch the ball without moving it, but this was only by learning exactly how far to stretch, not by judging the distance and getting it right. As soon as he told her to speed up she started over-reaching again. She stopped and felt for her keyboard.

'Got two arms,' she said.

'Sure, like everyone else. Only your other one's supposed to be still asleep.'

'No. Two this side.'

'Right. They told me you might, only I didn't want to put the idea into your mind. One's a sort of ghost, uh?'

36

Eva grunted. That was exactly the word. Ghost. The ghost of a human arm still trying to work, to reach and touch at the mind's command. You couldn't see it but it was there, moving slightly out of synch as the chimp arm moved, with the elbow wrong and the invisible fingertips wavering among the chimp knuckles. When she closed her eyes she saw in her mind the pale slim fingers, helpless, trapped in this strange hairy place, lost. Mustn't think like that. Mustn't.

'Want to give it a rest?' said Robbo.

She grunted a No, and this time as soon as he'd steadied the ball she snaked her arm out, fast as she could move it, not giving her mind time to think about the task. She missed, but by less than a centimetre.

'Not bad,' said Robbo.

After a few more tries he gave her a moving target by swinging the ball around, at first in a clean pendulum-curve, then in a circle, and finally making it jiggle as it swung.

'Tired, I guess.'

'You came along j...

know. Few more weeks and I'd have been out of a job.'

'Uh?'

'That's right. Ten years ago, when I went into this, I reckoned I was set up for life. Don't mean I thought we'd be actually colonizing planets before I died, but the push would be there, the pressure to get off-earth, and at least that'd mean research for us in the business. But now, look, they're all giving up. The pressure's still there, but the governments are pulling out and the sponsors are pulling out and whole departments are closing down. At Space-tech alone we've lost forty per cent of our jobs in the last three years.'

Eva clicked commiseration. Robbo went on talking, as much to give her a rest as anything.

'I don't know. It just doesn't make sense. There's no reason to it. It's like we've just given up. We're tired of trying. I worry about my kid, what life's going to be like for him . . .'

He got out his wallet and showed Eva a photograph of a little boy, pretty as himself with the same glossy brown skin and dark eyes. He went on talking. Eva half-listened. People, she thought – they're funny. Her fingers moved caressingly over the furriness of her chest, and somehow the thought in her mind changed from the oddness of people worrying about why they'd stopped trying to colonize planets to the oddness of people not having any proper hair on their bodies, being so smooth and shiny. When she thought of him like that Robbo didn't seem pretty at all.

'Try something else?' he said at last. She grunted OK and he swung her table across the bed and gave her some coloured bricks to build a tower with. She made it straight and slim, and far higher than a chimp could ever have done. Not that chimps are clumsy – they pick and groom among each other's fur with nimble, sensitive fingers – but they don't think tidy. Give them a cylinder to fit into a hole and they'll fumble it in any old how because that's good enough. It wouldn't enter their heads to square up the edges of a pile of blocks, so they'd get it out of kilter and down it would crash. But Eva could use her human mind to tell the chimp fingers what she wanted, and check by touch that they'd got it right. When Robbo asked her to speed it up she became chimp-clumsy. By that time she was tired again, so Robbo chatted a bit more and left.

She lay with her eyes shut, but as soon as she began to feel drowsy she forced them open and pressed the keys on her control box.

'Don't want to sleep,' said her voice.

'Just as you like, lovey,' sighed Meg's soft answer from behind the bedhead.

Wakefulness came flooding back, and Eva reset the mirror to show her the window, with a rainy mild day beyond the glass. There were dull grey clouds touching the tops of the dull grey towers, and air in the distance like smoke where the rain fell dense. She felt

closed, stirring

get rid of that ghost.

It was important. It was more important than just for walking without falling flat on your face. The thing is, you aren't a mind *in* a body, you're a mind *and* a body, and they're both *you*. As long as the ghost of that other body haunted around her she would never become a *you*, belonging all together, a whole person. She could probably learn how to pick things up cleanly and pour out of a bottle and run around without tripping by training herself not to notice the ghost, but it would be there still. No good.

She wondered whether to talk to Mrs Alonso about this. Mrs Alonso was all right, but Eva had rather taken against her. She was too kind, too cooing, it wasn't real. While she sat smiling by the bed Eva kept seeing Mrs Alonso II, tucked out of sight in the corner of the room, thin-lipped, scribbling notes for a scientific article. Anyway, she didn't actually *know* anything – nobody did, because Eva was the first of her kind and it was all new to everyone – but at least the biochemists and neurologists and everythingelsists knew a few facts about brains and bloodstreams and nervous systems and so on, but the psychiatrists were guessing all the way. Eva thought she could guess just as well as Mrs Alonso.

So, now, she closed her eyes again and summoned up the dream. She lay wide awake, concentrating with all her will but letting the images float into her mind, the shapes of a green tree world, branches with bark rough or smooth, blobs and patches of sunlight seeping through the leaf-cover, fruits and berries yellow, green, purple, orange, and through all this a single person, a body completely itself with its own mind part of it and the body part of the mind, reaching, grasping, swinging below a branch, finding and holding with a foot, reaching on.

Kelly was dead, gone, would never come back, but something was still there. Not a particular chimp with particular memories of a large cage with a

40

cement floor and a steel-and-plastic climbing frame and perhaps a human who took her out to greener places on a lead, but a chimp still, with older, deeper memories. You couldn't just invade a chimp body and take it over with your human mind, like a hero in a history book – you'd never get to be whole that way. Eva's human neurones might have copied themselves into Kelly's brain, but as Dad had said that left a sort of join, an interface, a borderland where human ended and chimp began. You couldn't live like that, with a frontier in you, like a wall, keeping your selves apart. The only way to become whole was to pull the wall down, to let the other side back in, to let it invade in its turn, up into the human side, the neurones remembering their old paths, twining themselves in among the human network until both sides made a single pattern. A new pattern, not Eva, not Kelly – both but one.

That must be why she'd started dreaming the _____ even before she had first woken. The chimp _____ find its way back. So now, _____ closed

that unless she _____
Inside her hairy skull she let the _____ real. It was peaceful, endless, happy. There were no humans in it.

MONTH TWO, DAY NINETEEN

Awake . . .
Not just your eyelids rising, facing the day . . .
Your whole body, all of it, moving and feeling . . .

Carefully Eva pushed herself off the pillow and sat.
With her right arm she heaved the bedclothes aside,
then twisted herself till her legs dangled over the edge.
All wrong. She was thinking too much. This was how
a human would try to get out of bed, unaided for the
first time, after a long illness. The ghost was very
strong. All the shapes and distances seemed strange.
Mum was watching from the chair.

'Sure you don't want me to help?' she said.

Eva rippled her fingers over the keyboard which
now lay strapped to her chest. After her weeks of
practice she'd got the pauses down to only a couple
of seconds.

'I'm fine,' she said. 'Been doing my exercises.'

A chimp wouldn't have got up like this. It would
have sort-of rolled, and then dropped. She dropped.
The ghost had judged the distance wrong, but her real
limbs got it right and she didn't stagger. She climbed
into Mum's lap, giving her time to adjust the half-
dozen sensor-wires she still had to trail around before
she kissed her. Mum laughed.

'It's like being eaten alive,' she said.

Eva made her No-it's-not grunt. A proper chimp-kiss is done with the mouth wide open, but she'd done hers human style, though admittedly she'd produced more suck than she'd meant to. She settled against Mum's shoulder and without thinking lifted her hand and started to pick with inquisitive fingers among the roots of the grey-streaked hair. She felt Mum stiffen, and then try to relax.

'You won't find anything, darling,' she said.

The chimps in the Research Section of the Pool were allowed a few harmless parasites so that they could have the satisfaction of catching them in their endless grooming sessions, but a flake of dried skin or a scrap of dirt would do almost as well. That wasn't the point.

'Mm-hmmm,' Eva murmured on a rising note.

Mum twitched and relaxed again.

'Don't tease,' she said. 'I'm not in the mood.'

Eva shrugged her shoulder forward and said, 'You ____. It's kind of comforting.'

____ ____ ____ ____ you don't go poking in my ear-

thing to be done ____ ____ about her fingertips as they work ____ the fur. All the same it was lovely to be able to feel the movement after the weeks of stillness and numbness. If she'd been a cat, Eva would have purred.

'I'm supposed to be talking to you,' said Mum.

43

'Uh?'

'Have you thought about the sort of life you're going to live when you're up and about?'

'Lots. Skiing's going to be fun.'

The snow-peaks and the beaches were almost the only human playgrounds left. There wasn't a lot else you could do with them. Mum chuckled.

'My legs are going to be so strong,' said Eva. 'And I can get my centre of gravity right down. I could be a world-beater. How'd you like to have a famous daughter?'

'Not much. People are going to be a bit interested in you anyway, darling. You know how they are about chimps as it is.'

'They'll get used to me. Anyway, I want to be ordinary – go back to school, be with Bren and Ginny . . . They came round last night, you know?'

'They said they might . . . I'm afraid there's a bit more to it than that, darling.'

'Uh?'

'Haven't you wondered where the funds have come from for all this?'

Mum tilted her head to show she meant the room, and the machines, and the control-room beyond, and so on.

'Research, I guess.'

'Of course, but research still has to be funded. Dad and I couldn't have afforded it, and the Pool's got nothing to spare. Joan may be famous, but she's still got to get her funds from somewhere. What she did, in fact, was set up a sort of arrangement with SMI – you know, the shaper people – and they raised the money from some of their advertisers who were interested. World Fruit's the main one, I believe.'

'You mean I'm *sponsored*!'

Eva used the keyboard to make such a squeak of outrage that Mum laughed aloud.

'I'm afraid so, my darling. You weren't available on public service.'

'Grrgh!'

'And of course this means that SMI are going to want to do at least one programme about you. There are other things, like World Fruit having an option for you to appear in some of the Honeybear commercials . . .'

'Uh?'

'They can't *make* you, if we don't agree, but you aren't allowed to advertise anyone else's products – that's what an option means.'

'Might be fun. And *lot* of grapes.'

'Is that all you can think of? I'm trying to explain that quite soon SMI are going to start wanting some while you were

'Have I got to.

'Well, yes, at least one. That's in the contract that . . . You see, *if* people are interested in you, enough of them, then that's going to mean more programmes, and that's going to mean money coming in, not just for you and Dad and me – I mean it'd be nice, but we don't really . . . You see, we actually *owe* Joan, morally I mean, for what she's done. Then there's the Pool . . .'

Mum sighed. The Pool was always desperate for funds. It was a fact which Eva had grown up with, almost like the laws of gravity.

'OK,' she said. 'If it's for the Pool.'

'I knew you'd say that.'

'Provided they don't try and make out I'm some kind of freak.'

A pause. Mum sort-of squaring her shoulders, inside.

'There's bound to be a bit of that, darling. I mean, we've got to get used to the idea that people are going to stare. Some people. I suppose in the long run it's going to be up to you to show them you're not.'

In her skiing fantasy Eva had imagined the gawps of the other skiers as she careered down the slopes. And school – of course heads would turn when she first came into class, but kids get used to things pretty quickly. She hadn't really thought about living her life as the object of an endless stare. People!

No, you didn't have to have people, not all the time.

'OK,' she said. 'And when it gets too much, I can always go and join the Pool and be a chimp for a bit.'

She felt Mum's body stiffen beneath her, as if she'd got cramp. Eva thought she'd just been keeping the conversation going, but now . . . yes, better get it said. It was important.

'It's all right, Mum. I'll only go to the Reserve.'

'Are you serious?'

'Mind you, if I went to a Public Section, people

46

wouldn't know which one was me. I'd have to take my clothes off, of course.'

'*Please*, darling . . .'

'It's all right, Mum.'

'Let's talk about something else.'

That was family code, just like a chimp-code, only in words – a way of not getting into a row. You chose another subject and hoped the row would simply go away, like a headache – only this one, Eva knew, wasn't going to, but for now she obeyed the code.

'What about clothes then?' she said.

'Yes, we've got to sort that out. Have you got any ideas?'

'Bow in my hair?'

Mum managed a laugh. She'd always loved making clothes for her pretty daughter. The chimps in the Pool mostly wore nothing, but were dressed in child's overalls when Dad took them on expeditions, partly because they weren't house-trained and had to use ~~nappies,~~ but mainly to hide the sexual swellings on ~~which~~ people who didn't

'I suppose so.'

'I'm not going to try and look human.'

Silence, but Eva could feel the sigh.

'It's important, Mum. I've got to be happy with this new me, and so've you. Not just think it's better than me being dead. Happy to have me like this.'

47

'I'm trying, darling. I really am trying.'

Poor Mum. It was much harder for her. When you're born you get imprinted with your mother's face, and she with yours. It happens with a lot of animals, some more strongly than others. With humans it's about middling, but the bond is still there, deep inside you, hard to alter. Eva still had the same Mum she'd always known, but Mum had this new thing, this stranger, this changeling. She couldn't help yearning in her depths for her own daughter, the one with the long black hair and blue eyes and the scar on her left ear lobe where a chimp had bitten her when she was three. However much she taught herself to think of this new Eva as that daughter, it wasn't the same as feeling she was.

It was unfair to push her too hard. Eva stopped grooming Mum's hair and took her hand and held it, human-style. Mum squeezed back, but let go. Eva's was not the hand she needed, not any longer. It was long and bony-fingered with hair on the back. How could anyone pretend it was her daughter's?

And, Eva knew, Mum was trying harder than anyone else would, ever.

MONTH TWO, DAY TWENTY-FIVE

Awake.
Standing by the window, looking down, nerve-ends
*   electric . . .*
Like standing on a cliff-top, imagining falling . . .
Falling into the world, people, people, people . . .
Having to move among them, to begin to live . . .

'Big day,' said Robbo.

Eva turned at the sound of his voice. He stood smiling at the door, handsome as a shaper-cop. His skin glistened like a fresh nut. He was wearing a brand-new outfit, straight from the shops, with fawn trousers moulded to his legs and a loose fawn jacket

ing?'

'You want me to do *tricks*?'

She didn't get the sneer quite right. Practising when you were alone wasn't the same as talking, and she still made mistakes. Robbo was used to it and hardly noticed, but from today on it mattered. People judge other people by their voices. If you sound stupid you are stupid. If you don't sound real, you aren't – you're not a person.

'I've seen chimps walking,' said Robbo. 'Of their own accord.'

'When they've got something to carry. Like I've seen humans crawling.'

'OK, OK, walk how you want. Let's go and look at this gym, uh? They've just about got it finished in time.'

He turned and held the door for Eva as if going through it was the most ordinary thing you could think of. Last evening, while Dad and Joan and Ali and Meg and the rest of the team had stood round, Doctor Richter had ceremonially removed the last pair of sensor cables that tied her to the machines. Champagne corks had popped. Everyone had wished her good luck. And today she was free. Going through the door was like being hatched, coming out of her safe egg into the huge world.

The world was a shambles. First there was a little empty vestibule, and beyond that the control room, where new machines were being uncrated, technicians were arguing over a wiring diagram, a supervisor was frowning at a print-out. Eva knuckled through the mess beside Robbo and out into a wide hospital corridor. She was glad now of the boring exercises he and the physics had made her do all the last seven weeks. She felt none of the tiredness and heaviness you'd have expected after all that time in bed – in fact an exhilarating lightness filled her, becoming stronger and stronger, until she lost control and went scampering on ahead, hooting with pleasure as she ran.

Then she stopped dead, with all the hairs along her back prickling erect. Her call had been answered, not with the same call, but with a series of short breathy barks on a slightly rising note, snapped off into silence. A chimp call. Eva had never heard it before, but she knew, or rather she felt, what it meant. *Alone*, it said. *Lost. Frightened. Where are you?* She felt the answer rising in her throat, but suppressed it as Robbo caught up with her.

'Who's that?' she said.

'Who's what?'

The call began again while Eva was still pressing keys. *Alone. Lost . . .*

'That, you mean?' said Robbo. 'Next patient, I guess. Now Prof Pradesh has proved she can do it with you . . .'

'They're going to do *lots*?'

(Kelly after Kelly after Kelly?)

'Sure. Got to try again, haven't they? Check it all ~~out? That's~~ how science works. You want to be the

the human mind. It couldn't stop

mind. Once it found one thing out, it had to move on. And *then*, what? it kept saying. You do one experiment and it works, so you try it again, with a difference, to see if that works too. And again, and again . . . So there wasn't just one chimp shut up, lonely, frightened, bewildered, having its blood sampled, its brain-rhythms measured, all that. Eva's control room was having new gadgets moved in so it could take care of more than one experiment . . .

'Now, what do you think of that!'

'Hoo!'

'Who what?'

'OK, who paid for it?'

'You can't read?'

Eva looked again. The gym wasn't large, but it shone like a glossy new toy, and smelt of fresh plastic and varnish. In one corner a shaper crew were rigging lights and a camera. There was a climbing frame, a trapeze, a vaulting horse and a lot of moveable kit, and every item, she now saw, had the Honeybear logo on it. Eva knew it so well that she hadn't noticed it. Because Honeybear used chimps in their ads there'd always been free Honeybear drinks at home, ever since she could remember. Now there was a free gym. OK.

She knuckled across the floor and swung herself up into the frame.

'Hey! Take it easy!' said Robbo. 'Don't want you breaking a rib. We should've had a week, at least, trying out what you can do before they did the programme. Watch it!'

Impossible to obey. It was so glorious to be moving like this, reaching, grasping, swinging across. She knew she was still only about half-strong, despite the exercises – when she was fully fit a grown man would have trouble holding her – but now what mattered was the sheer pleasure of movement, the feeling of naturalness. This was what these arms, these fingers,

were for. It mattered because it allowed her to understand the rightness of this new body, to feel its beauty
and energy . . .

'Watch it, I said!' snapped Robbo.

Eva squatted into a crook of the frame and hooted
derisively, but in fact he'd been right. For a moment,
quite unpredictably, the ghost of a human arm had
flickered into her mind, making her miss her grip,
have to grab with the other hand, clutch. The ghost
came back even more strongly when she tried the
swing. Long ago, as a small girl, that body had learnt
the to-and-fro rhythm, the exact timing needed to
fling her weight on the chains and drive the swing forward through its arc. This body was differently
weighted. Its arms were the wrong length. The
rhythm wouldn't come. Thinking didn't help, because
the old human timing was imprinted below the level
of thought, putting a jiggle into the arc and spoiling
the acceleration. Swinging was something she'd have
to learn fresh.

cles. She was wobbling along
pedal-movement when some people came out of a
door just ahead of her, not looking where they were
going because the man in front was talking over his
shoulder. Trying to miss him Eva steered into the wall
and crashed. That stopped their talk.

She picked herself up and saw that the man she'd missed was a stranger, though there was something familiar about him all the same. If he hadn't been wearing heavy dark glasses she might have recognized him. The people he'd been talking to over his shoulder were Dad and Joan Pradesh and a nervous-looking young woman. Eva rippled her fingers over the keys.

'Hi, Dad. Got to learn all over fresh.'

'Better learn to look where you're going.'

'This is her?' said the stranger.

'This is Eva,' said Joan. 'This is Dirk Ellan, Eva. I'm sure you've seen him on the shaper.'

Eva grunted a greeting. The man just nodded, not to her but to Joan, telling her Yes, he'd seen this chimp. Something about the nod made the name click. Dirk Ellan! Of course, though Eva hadn't watched his programmes often. Dad had taught her to be scornful of the sort of predigested science you got on the shaper.

'We were coming to see how you were getting along,' said Dad.

'She's been doing fine, Dr Adamson,' said Robbo. 'Times you wouldn't know she wasn't a chimp. Few things she can't handle yet.'

'Like riding a bike,' said Dad.

He was smiling inside his beard. Too much. Eva wasn't surprised at the way Robbo had hurried to get his word in, but Dad! All anxious and eager. And Mr Ellan's nods and silences showed that he was used to this sort of reaction – expected it in fact. It was just like the chimps in the Pool, with their boss-males, and the other males constantly making special signals to placate or challenge the bosses. Eva didn't remember noticing humans behaving like this in the old days, but now everything the three men did seemed obvious, a language she'd always known.

Back in the gym she climbed and swung a bit, to show them what she could do. Then there was a long wait while the shaper people set the cameras up, and discussed angles, and changed their minds, and argued. Then she went through her paces; first, things chimps could do naturally, like climbing and swinging; then things they might be taught to do, like riding a bike; and then things they couldn't, like building a self-supporting arch of toy bricks. There were long waits between each take.

Eva needed the rests. She was still only half-strong, and tired quickly. So she sat hunkered into a fork of the climbing frame and watched the others, Dad trying to impress Mr Ellan, Joan ignoring the hustle and working at some problem on scraps of paper, Robbo chatting up one of the shaper-women. Sometimes a

away hoot. The whole gym-run turned
startled as they were, Eva shrugged, grinned and waved a hand. Forget it. They forgot it and went on with what they'd been doing.

When she'd done enough tricks to keep them happy Mr Ellan came over and leaned against the frame beside Eva. His whole personality changed as the cameras closed around the pair of them. He'd taken his dark glasses off, letting the world see the smile-lines crinkling at the corners of his eyes. He was relaxed, friendly, trustworthy, understanding – all that. Eva knew it was just his job, a performance, but all the same she felt her skin unprickle.

'So you're Eva?' he said.

'And you're Dirk Ellan.'

'Right. I better explain to viewers there's got to be that little blip while that gismo you've got puts the words together for you. And just in case there's some real meanies out there, thinking it's all a trick, how about you spelling out something real slow, so we can show 'em it just ain't so?'

Eva grunted, eased the keyboard from its loops and held it so that a camera could watch while with one thin dark finger she pressed the individual keys.

'You've got it wrong, you meanies.'

She rewound the little tape and played the words several times, varying the tone of voice.

'That's amazing,' said Mr Ellan. Eva thought she could just hear a flicker of real surprise under the easy public accent. Perhaps he'd been wondering too – why not? Anyway, he was a meany himself, in spite of the signals. Deliberately she gave him a genuine chimp snicker. His eyebrows went up.

'But inside there you're really a young woman?' he said.

'I'm Eva OK.'

He didn't seem to notice her answer wasn't the same as 'Yes'. He wouldn't.

'And how exactly does it feel?'

Eva managed to suppress another snicker. This was one of Dad's bugbears – 'And how *exactly* does it feel, Mrs Hrumph, to have your husband reveal he's a practising werewolf?' – but she'd promised herself she was going to be on her best behaviour. The programme was important for everyone, especially the Pool. The trouble was that Mr Ellan filled her with a spirit of mischief – and *that* wouldn't have been there in the old days, either.

'It feels great,' she said. 'I'm looking forward to things.'

'No regrets?'

'No regrets.'

'I've seen pictures of you. You used to be a very pretty little miss. How about that?'

Eva glanced at him. He was horrible. Didn't he realize Mum would be watching? She wanted to bite his ear off. No. But she'd get him somehow.

'I'm very pretty now,' she said.

'Sure, but . . .'

a real smacker, maximum vacuum. He was still trying to push her clear when she let go. He backed off while she sat laughing in the nook of the frame. He managed a sort of laugh too, but she could see the fright and fury in his eyes, just as she could feel the various reactions from the dimness beyond the camera-lights, pleasure and alarm and excitement all mixed together. The shaper people, they must know he was a meanie. By the sound of their laughter, they did.

'Gee, you're strong,' he said.

'Chimps are.'

'But you're supposed to be a young woman.'

'I'm a chimp too. And I like it.'

'Sure, sure.'

PART TWO
LIVING

MONTH FOUR, DAY TWELVE

Living at home, at last . . .
But the ghost still there . . .
The ghost moving about these rooms . . .
Making herself snacks in this kitchen . . .
Gazing, now, out of this window . . .

There was a particular moment sometimes when the sun went down. It needed the right weather, a cloudless sky and a mild west wind to clear the brownish haze of the city. Then for a few moments below the earliest stars and above the still-faint pattern of city lights you might just catch a different kind of glimmer, a wavering thread, the twinkle of snow on

The ghost had been particularly ~~strong~~ing, because of being home and waking in her own bed. Eva had woken on the edge of horrors, desperate for the feel of her own long-limbed smooth-skinned body, her own hair to brush, her own teeth to clean, her own dark blue eyes to ring with

61

eyeshadow. Dad had had to give her an extra shot of the dope she still took to suppress that kind of feeling, so perhaps that was why the ghost that yearned for the ski-slopes was now only a vague shadow in her mind, and Eva, the new Eva, the one she must learn to think and feel of as the only real Eva, was merely amused and interested at the idea of going skiing. She might have been excited if Dad had announced they were off to the mountains next weekend, but she didn't yearn any more. That kind of intense, shapeless longing was for something else.

What?

The answer came when she closed her eyes. Leaves mottling the dark behind the eyelids. Trees. Only where could you still find trees, real trees in forests, the way you could still find mountains?

Up north, in the timber-stands, grown as a thirty-year crop? No good. The branches were the wrong shape to swing through or nest among. You couldn't live in those winters. You couldn't eat pine needles. South, then? There were bits of jungle still – you saw them sometimes on the shaper. Nearly three thousand miles on beyond the mountains, there were five or six valleys which had never been cleared, where the rain-forest trees still grew and the lianas dangled. There were a few other places in the world like that, tiny preserved patches, most of them funded by the shaper companies, studied and guarded by scientists, kept free from other human intrusion. But perhaps Dad might be able to arrange something, a research project which needed a sort-of-chimp to be in a jungle for a bit . . .

It was a fantasy, and Eva knew it. It was a way of

dreaming the dream. She kept her eyes closed and let it happen. Unnoticed beside her the ghost thinned, dwindled, vanished.

Bip. Bip. Bip. Mum had no sense of time, so she set the kitchen timer for anything that mattered. Its shrill sound stopped and Mum came into the living room and switched on the shaper. A holiday ad filled the zone, bronze bodies on a pale beach, ridiculously less crowded than a real beach would be. Mum settled into her chair and Eva knuckled over and climbed into her lap. Mum laughed resignedly.

'I suppose we've got to watch,' she said.

'Dad's big day.'

Eva was glad she'd made enough fuss to force them to let her come home in time to watch the programme with Mum. It wouldn't have been fair on Mum to make her watch it alone. Dad was down at the studios, because part of the format of Mr Ellan's programmes was always a live discussion. Mum could have come to the hospital to watch, of course, but that would

sequence had been taken ...

Mum stiffened and closed her eyes. Mr Ellan's solemn half-whisper began as a voice-over.

'This girl's name is Eva. Just over a year ago she was involved in a car accident and suffered extensive physical damage. She would certainly never have walked, let alone skated, again. Furthermore she was in an irreversible coma. Yet today Eva is alive, active, healthy. She looks, however, quite different. She looks like *this*.'

And there was Kelly, squatting among the yellow bars of the climbing frame. She pursed her lips forward and hooted. *Go away* – but to humans it would be just a hoot, and anyway she immediately shrugged, grinned and waved a friendly hand. Eva stared. Me, she thought. Me. Though she was used by now to looking at her own image in a mirror and accepting it as herself, the chimp in the zone was like a stranger. The brown eyes were bright with cleverness and mischief. The big ears stuck out through the coarse black hair. Eva felt a rush of friendliness and liking, and without thinking started a silent pant of greeting. Faintly she was aware of the old Eva gazing through her eyes, dismayed, trying to make the lips and throat cry *No!*, but thanks to the dope it wasn't difficult to blank her out and will a *Yes* with her conscious mind. She glanced up, wanting to share that *Yes*. Mum still had her eyes shut.

'Try and watch, Mum,' she made the keyboard murmur. 'It's me now. We've got to like this me. I do already. Really. I'm not pretending.'

'I'm so glad, darling.'

'I know it's harder for you.'

'I'll learn.'

The climbing frame vanished, leaving Kelly hanging in mid-air as a still. The girl in the yellow tracksuit appeared on the opposite side of the zone, and Mr Ellan strolled up between them as though he'd just happened along.

'In the next hour,' he said, 'we are going to show you the full story of this astonishing event. Before we begin I should point out that but for the generosity of Honeybear Soft Drinks it would not have been possible. Eva's transformation was a very expensive procedure, demanding the attention of many highly-skilled scientists working at the very frontier of technology. Such work does not come cheap, and Eva and her parents have cause to be very grateful indeed to Honeybear for their help. We have with us in the studio this evening one of those parents, Doctor Daniel Adamson of the International Chimpanzee Pool . . .'

The zone widened and there was Dad, smiling at the cameras, his blue eyes bright in the studio lights, his whole face and attitude saying *Like me, oh, please like me*.

'. . . and we are also honoured to have with us Professor Joan Pradesh, whose work in the field of neurone memory, first discovered by her father, made

sound on. You've g

Eva grunted a yes. She didn't mind – she could listen later too. And meanwhile it was interesting to watch Dad trying to tell Mr Ellan how *exactly* . . . And then there was a picture of Dad's car lying upside-down with its roof caved in; and then a shape on a hospital bed, a mound of bandages with tubes running in and out – Mum had her eyes shut again – and then the same shape, with a sort of box like a coffin beside it. The cameras closed in to a little window in the lid of the box. Dimly, behind the glass, you could see something that might have been a dark, furry head with its eyes closed . . .

Eva was glad they had the sound off. There was something holy about the silent pair, something you didn't want Mr Ellan, or even Dad, telling you what to think about . . . But it was interesting that they'd started making the programme even then, so that Honeybear could have something to pay for. It must all have cost the earth, Eva realized. They'd be wanting to see returns on their money from now on.

'It's all right, you can look now. It's Joan,' she said, switching up the sound.

Joan was pure Joan, despite the mauve dress, looking and sounding as if she thought the programme was a complete waste of her time. She didn't even try to make things easier for the dimwits out there watching, but Mr Ellan was pretty good at his job, really, asking his questions in a way which forced her to give the dimwits a chance. They'd only been going a few minutes when the commo beeped. Mum picked it up with her free hand.

'Hello. Who? Oh, no. No, I don't want to talk about it. No thank you.'

She rang off.

'A woman from some other programme,' she said. 'How did they get our new number? It isn't on the . . .'

The commo beeped again. She picked it up, said

Hello, listened for a moment and rang off. Eva reached over and switched it to autocall.

'. . . that Eva was used to chimps?' Mr Ellan was saying. 'From what Doctor Adamson was telling us she'd practically grown up with them.'

The zone showed another amateur sequence, a naked human child with blue eyes and dark hair playing absorbedly in a sandpit. A half-grown female chimp knuckled into view and started to search intently across her scalp. The child seemed hardly to notice.

'I can only say it *may* have been of importance,' Joan said. 'The brain is an extremely complex mechanism, and we do not yet understand many things about it. In this case the problems of rejection in the immediately post-transferral stage may well have been eased by experiences analogous to maternal imprinting in Eva's early childhood. However . . .'

The doorbell rang. One of the neighbours, thought Eva, checking we know the programme's on – people ⌐ldn't use the commo because ⌐ Thanks

their ID cards ⌐ lintel. They were calling out ⌐ because the volume was off. Behind them the lift doors opened and more people jostled out, some with cameras.

'I knew this was going to happen,' said Mum.

'Jerry swore he wouldn't let anyone through the main doors, but I just knew.'

'How'd they get here so soon?' said Eva. 'I thought . . .'

'SMI did a lot of publicity. They guaranteed no one would be told our name in advance, but somebody at the studios must have sold it to the other companies. Shaper people will do *anything*.'

The doorbell was ringing now without stopping. People were banging at the door itself. It was supposed to be break-in-proof, but you couldn't be sure. Mum pressed a couple of keys and spoke into the mouthpiece of her control.

'This is Mrs Adamson. We are not giving any interviews. Will you please go away. You are trespassing on private property.'

Nothing happened. Perhaps they hadn't heard through the racket they were making, hammering and calling and swearing at each other and pressing the bell. Even from right inside the flat the noise was loud enough to feel dangerous. More people came out of the lift. Mum repeated her message. And again, and again. The doorbell stopped. Now they were shouting at each other not to shout at each other, and making shushing gestures. Then silence. You could see they could hear the message because half a dozen microphones poked up towards the speaker to record Mum's voice. It didn't do any good. The bell started again at once, and the shouting and knocking.

Now the door on the other side of the landing opened and little Mr Koo came out to complain about the racket. The Koos never watched the shaper, so he couldn't have understood what was happening, but the moment they saw him the reporters closed round him like wasps attacking a caterpillar, yelling questions and thrusting microphones and cameras at him. He retreated, but before he could close the door they surged in round him, leaving room on the landing for the lift to disgorge another load, and these newcomers, seeing their rivals streaming through an open door, must have thought the Adamsons lived that side and pressed in after them while the poor old lift went down for yet another load.

White and shuddering Mum plugged the commo in. It immediately started to beep, but after several tries she hit a clear space and got a channel out. She called the police, but whoever she spoke to said they couldn't help. Then she tried the home number of a man she knew in the police department, because of her job, and he said the same, explaining privately that the police never interfered with shaper people if they could help it because the shaper people always got their own back by putting on programmes

the coat-cupboard, jumped, g
self up. Crouching on top of the door, clutching it with her feet, she inspected the box. There wasn't a switch, but there was a grille in front through which the sound came, so she swung down and fetched a packet of rice from the kitchen. Using the lid of the

packet as a sort of chute she eased a stream of rice into the grille until the noise stopped.

She didn't come down at once. She felt safer, crouched up there, away from the floor. The voices from beyond the door made her fur prickle, and her throat and lips worked involuntarily, wanting to shout back. Though she couldn't hear any words the voices still had a meaning – they were hunting cries, the calls of a pack, baying outside the lair of its prey. Of course if they'd been let in the people out there wouldn't have hurt her, only asked stupid questions. That was what her mind told her. But her body told her they were enemy. It was an effort to climb down and go back into the living room.

Mum was still white and shivering.

'Hadn't we better call Dad?' said Eva, using the tone control on her keyboard to sound calm.

'The programme's still on. He'll be in the studio.'

'You better warn him. He'll never get in.'

Again it took several tries to get a channel out, but in the end Mum managed to find someone who said they'd tell Dad as soon as they could.

'I never dreamed it would be as bad as this,' said Mum. 'I realized they'd be interested, but honestly! They're mad!'

No, they're just people, thought Eva. Time went by. The scrum on the landing calmed. The onslaught became a siege. Some of the attackers settled onto the floor and waited, others leaned against walls, a few spoke into pocket commos.

'Let's watch something else,' said Eva, taking the control and beginning to flick through the channels. The second one she came to was showing an old tape of chimps. She watched for a bit until she realized from the voice-over that it was a news programme, about her, only they didn't have anything to show the viewers except that tape. Three channels further on she found another news programme, live, with a reporter talking into camera in the street outside this very tower-block. Almost at once the shot switched to another angle, from far higher, this tower still, against the evening sky, with the city spreading on beyond it until it was lost in its own man-made dusky mist. The focus zoomed in to a particular window. The lights were on in the room, so you could just make out a woman sitting in a chair with a large dark something in her lap.

Mum sighed and pressed keys to lower the blind. In the imaged window in the zone the blind came down.

'Someone in one of the other towers must have let them use their flat,' said Mum. 'Honestly, people will do *anything*.'

People, people, people – even Mum talked as ___ she was people too. She ___der

aware of hear___ ___ she listened for them she knew that they muttering among themselves and gone quite silent. She switched the closed circuit on and saw that they were all standing up, facing the lift. She could hear the whine of its ascent.

'Dad,' said Mum. 'But he'll . . . how did they know?'

They had friends with commos below, of course, thought Eva, but she didn't have time to say so before the lift stopped and the gates opened. Two huge men in grey uniforms faced the crowd, who had begun to surge forward. They lowered their shoulders and charged out. Now Eva could see that there were four other people in the lift, Dad, a woman, and two more huge men in uniform. The crowd gave way before the charge but then surged in from the side as the second two guards tried to hustle Dad and the woman on through the gap. Dad looked terrified, though often you could hardly see him for out-thrust mircophones. The woman held herself very erect and spoke in a loud voice, clearly saying the same few words over and over. The guards elbow-jabbed the crowd aside. Eva saw at least one bleeding nose, and several people fell right over. When they reached the door the guards regrouped and kept the crowd at bay while Dad bent down to operate the voice-lock, but either because of the racket or because he was so scared his voice came out funny it didn't work at once, so Eva got there first and opened the door.

The crowd could barely have glimpsed her, but they let out a baying roar and surged forward as Dad and the woman slipped through. The guards just managed to hold them while Eva got the door shut.

Dad stood in the hall, shaking his head while the baying dwindled into shouts of pleading and frustration. He scuffed his toe at some of the rice Eva had spilt while she was silencing the bell.

'I didn't believe it,' he said. 'I just didn't believe it.'

'It is certainly far worse than anyone had expected,' said the woman, as calm as if she was discussing the weather. She was a bit over thirty, blonde, with fluffy hair and neat features. At first glance she looked rather fragile, despite her dark business suit, but she spoke and carried herself as though she wasn't afraid of anyone. She turned to Mum, who had come out into the hallway.

'Good evening, Mrs Adamson. I am Jane Callaway, from the legal and contract department of SMI. Before anything else I must apologize on behalf of the company for the intolerable disturbance you have suffered tonight.'

'It's awful,' said Mum.

'Let's have a drink,' said Dad.

'Just fruit juice for me,' said Miss Callaway. 'I'm working.'

Eva knuckled into the kitchen and got the drinks, making Dad's a bit stronger than usual. Miss Callaway said, 'Thank you' in a perfectly normal

the problems that arise in cases

'There can't be any cases like this!' said Mum.

'There are always unique features,' said Miss Callaway. 'That's why the public are interested. But the legal basis remains remarkably constant. In my experience your most straightforward course would be to assign exclusive rights in Eva's story to a company such as SMI. Part of the contract would be that we protected you from unwanted intrusion. As a private citizen you can't sue a reporter who tries to question you, but we can, because the reporter is asking you to break your contract with us. Now obviously you don't want to embark on a long-term contract without thinking it over, but in view of what has happened it would be a sensible course for you to assign the rights in the story over the next few days . . .'

She had opened her briefcase while she was speaking and pulled out a few sheets of paper. She continued to explain, cool, friendly, helpful. Eva stopped listening. There was something about the three of them, Mum and Dad and Miss Callaway, which puzzled her. Mum was frowning, Dad leaning forward in his chair, bright-eyed, nodding at each fresh point Miss Callaway made . . . This wasn't his sort of thing at all, but Mum though she wasn't a lawyer knew quite a lot about things like contracts, because her job often involved trying to help people who'd got into some kind of legal mess . . . Why was Dad so anxious? Why wasn't he trying to get his word in, as usual? Was it just that he was tired after the programme and still shocked by what had happened on the landing? Or . . .

Out of nowhere the thought floated into Eva's mind that Dad was acting. He already knew what Miss Callaway was going to say. He'd already talked to her about all this. And that meant . . .

No, he couldn't have known it was going to be like this. He hadn't been acting when he got home. He'd been really frightened, really shocked . . . But suppose

Miss Callaway's company *had* realized what was going to happen. Suppose they just allowed it to happen in cases like this, and then sent someone like Miss Callaway along, cool, friendly, helpful, while you had the reporter-pack actually baying on your doormat and all you could think of was getting rid of them. What they'd do was calm Dad down and get him to sort-of-agree not to worry till the time came, and tell him about the long-term contract and the kind of money that would be coming to the Pool, and he'd have sort-of-agreed to that too, and then sort-of-told them about Mum, and how she might react to the idea of assigning exclusive rights in her daughter's story to a shaper company . . .

Slowly Eva tapped a few words into her control box and waited for a pause before she pressed the 'Speak' key.

'Do you know who I belong to?'

The three heads jerked round.

'You don't belong to anyone, darling,' said Mum.

. . . but looked at Miss Callaway.

. . . when

before . . .

believe that when animals from the . . . are sold for research they are sold outright, and the organization doing the research then buys them. But in Eva's case, because the experiment was carried out by the Pool itself, in cooperation with the Pradesh

Institute, no such arrangement was made – in fact no arrangement was made at all.'

'I suppose I ought . . .' said Dad.

'There might therefore be an argument that Eva's body, at least, still belongs to the Pool.'

'This is ridiculous,' said Mum. 'Anyway, we could pay for her now – we'd have to find the money somehow.'

'The difficulty, Mrs Adamson, is that Eva is now an extremely valuable piece of property. The Trustees of the Pool might well argue . . .'

'She isn't property!'

'Well, I would agree that if the case were to go to court Eva would eventually be confirmed as a human being – that is to say not belonging to anyone but with her parents having the usual rights and responsibilities while she remains a minor. Even a point like that raises problems. How old is she? The human Eva is thirteen, but the body she is using is less than six. All I can tell you is that however the courts decided these points, the legal costs in coming to a decision might well prove very considerable indeed. That is why I have drafted a special clause into this contract under which my company accepts that Eva is fully human, with all that that implies, and furthermore the company undertakes in the event of your signing a long-term contract with us to bear all legal costs in arguing the case.'

'You got this all ready before?' said Mum.

Miss Callaway smiled, unruffled.

'It's my job to think of difficulties before they happen. The short-term preliminary contract I suggest is only one option. If you would like to discuss . . .'

'No. Let's have a look at it.'

Miss Callaway passed the papers across. Mum put on her specs and started to read. Dad beckoned to Eva. She knuckled across, climbed into his lap and started to finger through his beard.

'How did it go?' he muttered.

'Didn't have time to watch much. Joan had just started. Then *they* turned up.'

She shrugged a shoulder towards the doorway.

'But you've got it on tape?'

'Uh.'

They waited. Dad finished his drink. Miss Callaway sat still, patient as a hunter. At last Mum looked up.

'I suppose that's the best course,' she said. 'You really think you can get rid of them?'

'It has usually worked in the past,' said Miss Callaway, calm as ever – but then, for the first time, she gave a small jerk of surprise as Mum turned to Eva.

If Dad and I sign this it means that

They had

more slowly than usual, set her message, the words come slowly too.

'All right. Only provided you don't sign anything saying ordinary chimps belong to people either.'

She felt Dad's body jerk. Then he laughed his

infuriating little laugh which meant that what you'd just said was too silly to argue about.

'I don't think there's anything . . .' murmured Mum.

'No,' said Miss Callaway, 'and I will make a note to avoid phrases to that effect in future contracts. Now, if you will just sign here . . . and here, Doctor Adamson . . . excellent. And now I will see what I can do about driving the wolves from your door.'

She stood up, patted her hair smooth, and left. The racket from the landing rose as the door opened, then faded. Mum switched on the closed circuit to watch, but kept the volume off. Miss Callaway, flanked by security men, was reading a statement – she must have had that ready too. The camera only showed the back of her head. Microphones jutted towards her. The crowd were listening. Their faces signalled weariness, frustration, defeat. Some at the back were talking into commos. The lift doors were opening and several of the crowd were already waiting to board it. When Miss Callaway stopped reading, some questions were shouted, but she answered with a shake of her head. The lift went down, crammed. Miss Callaway came back into the flat and talked to Mum and Dad about an appointment to which they could bring their own lawyer. By the time she left the lobby was almost empty, and the guards were shoving the last few reporters into the lift by force. Two of the guards stayed on in case anyone tried to come back.

Eva woke several times in the night. She was oddly restless in her own bed. In the old days she used to sleep on her front, stretched right out, but now she felt more comfortable curled up. I'd really like a basket, she thought, a big dog-basket, like a nest. I wonder if Mum would mind. Perhaps if I told her I wanted a round patchwork, to cover it with . . .

Later she woke again and heard voices, Mum and Dad, Mum angry and hurt, Dad trying to talk his way out. They both hated rows, didn't even like arguments, Dad especially. It was typical he hadn't ever sorted out properly who owned Kelly, because that would have meant hassle. I'm going to have to watch Dad, Eva thought. Whatever he says, I'm going to see that I own me . . .

Another voice in the early dawn, only a murmur again, but unmistakable. Mr Ellan. Creeping out into the living room she found Dad settling down to watch his big moment. Since she'd missed so much with Mum turning the sound off and then the siege starting, she climbed into his lap to watch too. He welcomed her by ruffling the fur at the back of her head with easy fingers.

They watched the programme through to the end. It finished with a kiss. When Eva had grabbed Mr Ellan by the collar and given him that mighty, sucking smacker some cameraman had had the wits to zoom right in and get it in close-up. No professional

MONTH SIX, DAY TWO

Living with fame . . .

Studios, waiting for programmes to begin. Glare of shaper-lights. How-exactly-does-it-feel . . .?

Autographs (no good chimp-grip for a pen). Stares. Giggles.

Money and treats and meeting shaper-stars.

A bodyguard, Cormac, in case you got kidnapped. A secretary, Joe, to answer the commo and the post – journalists calling for a quick quote on Miss World or some diet fad, scientists wanting a slice of you (yes, a real slice sometimes, cells to culture, but usually only a slice of time and publicity) . . .

Dad getting offered visiting Professorships . . .

was over the Public Response Indicators were already registering high interest and excitement. That was why the reporters had been ringing at the door so soon. But if only she'd never kissed Mr Ellan. The PRI Index had really hit the roof then, they said. That's what the billions of watchers had really gone for.

Things that happened in their shaper zones were more solid to them, more important, more exciting than anything that happened in their own lives, and somehow that image – the chimp squatting among the yellow bars of the climbing frame, with the bright butterfly embroidered on her chest, and her glossy pelt and clear gaze, and then the great Dirk Ellan panicking in her grip, and the comic, huge-lipped kiss – people could never get enough of it. They had laughed, and fallen in love. The sequence was played again and again, and copied, and parodied, and referred to like a proverb everybody knew. On chatshows Eva had to cope with people trying to work themselves into a kiss-me position, so that they could share the effect. All the crammed world, even oddballs like the Koos who never watched the shaper, knew about Eva.

Fame could be useful. Mum and the school social worker, who'd been round several times to talk things over before Eva started school again, had been worried about how the other kids would react – whispers, giggles, stares, outright rejection perhaps. Eva herself had been pretty nervous first day, but in fact there was hardly any of that at all. She found she wasn't a stranger. The kids felt they already knew her, seeing her so often on the shaper in their own homes. Some of the smaller ones were into a craze for imitating her voice, fluttering their fingers across an imaginary keyboard on their chest and then speaking; some of them were so good Eva couldn't tell the difference. In most ways, too, kids were more sensible about fame than adults. The stares and the autographs lasted about a fortnight, only. A few of the little ones hung around longer, not because she was famous – not even thinking about that – but because they felt a need to touch and fondle and be happy with a furry creature. Left to herself Eva would probably have let it happen, but Ginny didn't like it and shooed the kids off.

Of course there'd been hours of talk about all this at home. Mum had had the main teachers round and they'd discussed everything they could think of, from security against kidnappers to having a special small desk, but still there'd been things they'd missed . . .

Eva was sitting hunkered on the low wall in the shade of the Language Block with Bren beside her and Ginny just beyond. Ginny was rabbitting away about why she was going to give Juan the push, and Bren, half jealous and half enjoying the idea of boys getting punished, was egging her on. A gang of juniors came shrieking round the corner of the block and Eva's pelt stirred uncomfortably at the sound, the massed voices of humans, the pack-cry. The whole air was full of the same noise, nearer and further, and

their own little bubble of privacy in a long, less kiss. Ginny had got round to describing Juan's eating habits and Bren was giggling at each fresh exaggeration. They didn't seem to notice the pressure either. It was as if you were born used to it, the clamour and the jostling, people, people, people. They were the air you breathed, the sea you swam in. But if you weren't people, you stifled, you drowned . . .

This feeling of pressure, of loneliness and strangeness in the crowd, was different from the sort of depression and sadness Eva still sometimes woke with, when she lay remembering how her old body used to enjoy lying in its bed, the caress of nightdress and warm sheets on smooth soft skin. She could take a shot of her dope when those ghost-feelings got too strong, though she didn't often need to, these days. But this was something else, a mirror-image, almost, not what the human part of her felt about being chimp, but what the chimp felt about being human.

The pressure rose as Ginny and Bren talked across her. Mostly they were very good, they tried hard, but when they got excited they forgot to include her in their glances. Anyway she wasn't interested in Juan. She shrank into herself, and as she did so became aware of a different ghost. It had no body, only a voice, the ghost of a cry, but so strong and near in her mind that every hair on her body stood out. She had heard it just once, weeks ago, when she'd been scampering along the hospital corridor to inspect her new gym, the call of a chimp, scared, lost and bewildered, and waiting – though it couldn't know it – to have its own mind emptied away so that a human mind could invade and explore human pathways through the now blank cells. Where was that chimp now, that mind, those memories? Where was Kelly? Lost . . . lost . . . lost . . .

She was moving before she understood what was happening. The violence of the reaction whirled her off through the gaps between the little knots of kids and then with a leap, clutch and swing up on to the shoulder of the old robed female statue – Mathematics or History or something – that stood by the Library steps. She crouched there in her blue overalls while the cry shuddered up through her. Lost . . . lost . . . lost . . . It echoed off the walls of the Language Block, the lonely cry of a ghost.

For a moment the clamour stopped. A couple of hundred heads turned to stare. Some of the kids laughed, and waved arms in greeting as though she was doing something clever. The mood died. She swung down and knuckled back to Bren and Ginny.

'What was that about?' said Bren.

'Did I say something stupid?' said Ginny, the same instant.

Eva made a forget-it grunt. A few minutes later the hooter sounded, calling the out-shift in to fill their heads with another ration of knowledge.

Eva went home on the school bus. There'd been a fuss
. . . wanted to send a car so

famous. Only it . . .
jams in the car lanes any faster, while the school bus could whisk her home in the bus lanes. How could you kidnap someone out of a bus on the bus lanes – you'd need to hijack another bus for a start . . .? Anyway, the company had given in in the end.

After Bren had got off Eva sat by herself, staring out over the endless lines of car-roofs, and at a jam-packed traveller, and the crowds on the pavement waiting for a gap to board it. People, people . . . They were strange, listless, empty. As if they didn't have anything to live for. Even Ginny and Bren, who seemed so lively, were only lively for today. They never thought about the future, or what was going to happen to them when they grew up. Their future was tomorrow, or next week, or next holiday . . .

Eva gazed at the people, full of a sense of not-belonging. She was as different from all of them as if she'd come from another planet, especially so today. Her outburst in the morning had left her both alarmed and exhilarated, which was strange, but she thought she knew why. Mum and Dad had taught her to loathe rows. You stayed calm, you bottled your anger up, if someone else was in a rage you kept clear of them, and if you did get into a row you felt sick about it for days – but that was the old Eva. Now there was Kelly too – not the old Kelly either. She was gone, with all her memories, all her sense of belong-ing and being herself in a particular time and place. She would never come back. But still she had left part of herself behind, her nature, her instincts, still root-ed deep into the body into which the human Eva had been grafted. That was the Kelly Eva herself had invited back across the shadowy border between mind and brain. She couldn't do that and then say OK, but I don't want all of her. I'll have the lightning reactions but not the tantrums, the warmth and fun but not the sullen hours, the sympathy but not the mischief. They were Eva too, now. She couldn't bottle them away . . . She remembered the relief that had washed through her after that outburst, and how she'd settled down at once to grooming Bren's hair. Just like a chimp in the pool after a fight. Of course.

Cormac met her at the bus stop, and she was glad to see him. He was huge and strong, very neat in his movements but simple-minded as a child. He thought of her as an animal, somebody's pet, and rumpled her pelt with absent-minded fingers and blinked with surprise when she spoke. Sometimes this was irritating, but today it was fine. Cormac knew the difference. She sat in the crook of his arm while they rode the traveller and then knuckled along in his wake for the last stretch. Cormac was big enough for people to stand out of his way, and the crowds, used to the little procession by now, would leave a space for Eva and say 'Hi!' to her as she passed, and she'd grin and wave a hand. Most days this was rather good, with its sense of acceptance, of friendliness from strangers,

longer than usual while he told Mum how well it had gone. Eva didn't listen much. There was something about Dad in his triumphant moods, though he was a pretty good lecturer – everyone said so . . .

'. . . interested to see how the next two experiments turn out,' he said, and took another mouthful.

In the pause Eva suddenly realized what he'd been talking about.

'Just two, Dad?'

'At the moment. Do you know, Joan's outfit has had more than sixty volunteers, last count?'

'How many chimps?'

'Nothing like enough. If we were to refuse any fresh research projects in other fields we might have seven candidates by the end of the year.'

'Seven volunteers?'

Dad had tried to stop the conversation by taking another mouthful.

'I heard a chimp calling in the hospital,' said Eva. 'First day I was right up. He didn't sound like a volunteer.'

'Caesar,' said Dad.

'How's he doing?'

'Too soon to say. Are you going to insist on discussing this, darling?'

'Please.'

'All right. As you know, I've never really liked the business of selling chimps for research and have always been very selective about projects. If it had not been for their research-value, there would be no chimps in the world today. If we didn't continue to sell the surplus, there would be no Pool.'

'Yes, I know, but . . .'

'But what?'

Now Eva wished she hadn't started. Her horror of talking about it like this made it difficult to think.

'This is different. You've saved my life but you've lost Kelly's. One chimp, one human. It isn't enough.'

'You mean that to justify the sacrifice of a chimp

one ought to be able to see the possibility of saving tens of thousands of human lives by the consequent research? I'd have to ask a philosopher if that made the difference. Let me put it another way. Suppose I went out sailing with my daughter and a young chimp, and the boat capsized, and I had the chance to save one of you but not both – you wouldn't expect me to save the chimp, would you?'

'I sometimes think so,' said Mum, meaning to make a joke of it but getting it wrong.

'Nonsense. It would be no choice at all. That was effectively the same decision we had to make about you. And then, if I can make it in your case, what right have I to withhold a similar chance from someone else? Suppose I were in my boat with a chimp and a stranger's child . . .'

'There's millions times more people than there's chimps,' said Eva.

It was an argument Eva'd heard him use himself, putting the case for more funds for his precious Pool.

You must have thought about

She could hear the wariness in his voice and tried to lighten her answer.

'A bit. I keep changing my mind. Your idea is we'll go along to the Pool and I'll choose a dishy male and you'll find some boy with an IQ of a hundred and

89

eighty who's just walked under a bus, and then Joan will put them together and we'll have a lovely wedding and live happily ever after?'

Dad laughed. Mum didn't.

'I hadn't got that far,' said Dad, but Eva had heard in the laugh and the silence that this was something they'd talked about, often.

'Our babies would be just chimps, wouldn't they?' said Eva. 'They'd be Kelly's, really.'

The tension-screw tightened another half turn. They'd talked about this, too. Dad chose to answer in his new voice, the shaper-scholar, patient but charming zoologist explaining to dimwits. Eva felt a prickle of irritation down her spine. He oughtn't to use that voice inside the family. It was his way, she guessed, of ducking the dangerous parts of her question (was she going to be allowed to have babies? If so, whose? How? With a real mate, or artificial insemination? And what a frenzy there'd be in the fame-market when it happened! The riot outside the flat the night of that first programme would be nothing compared!).

'That raises a very interesting point,' said Dad. 'Of course you're right in the sense that such a baby would inherit no human genetic material, but like humans chimps are not solely the product of their inheritance. They are also creatures of their own cultures, though to a lesser extent than humans. The literature about wild chimps shows that different groups had their different ways of doing things, using simple tools and so on, which the young learnt from their elders. Our own chimps would be lost if they had to return to a real jungle, because no one has taught them how to survive under such conditions, but on the other hand they have learnt new skills and social arrangements to cope with conditions in the Pool. The social conditions are specially important, because the restricted space has imposed a greater need for control of anti-social behaviour, and the successful males in particular are those with greater social skills and awareness. It is extremely hard to quantify, but I am beginning to believe that especially in the Reserve, where the natural selective process has most chance to operate, something very like an increase in intelligence is becoming perceptible . . .'

'But what about *my* babies?' said Eva.

'I was coming to that. The young of all higher animals are learning-machines. Evolution has programmed them to learn. The bigger brains they have, the more knowledge they can file and store. In all experiments with chimp-learning the teachers have been humans, apart from a few anecdotal instances

perhaps . . .

'Knots?'

'Knots is an excellent example. Knots require dexterity and intelligence, both at about the limit of natural chimp capacity. The brighter ones could tie knots, the less bright couldn't. Now suppose the ability to tie knots conferred an advantage in evolutionary terms, and suppose the knowledge of how to do it was passed on through a number of generations, then you would find that you had been breeding for dexterity and intelligence. You would have bred something into the chimp gene. A gift from humankind.'

Dad was really excited now, not just acting. His eyes sparkled and his beard wagged. If he'd had a mane of white hair he'd have been tossing it around. You couldn't help liking him in this mood, though Mum, Eva was aware, had switched right off and withdrawn into herself, as though all she could bear to think about was the process of cutting her food up on her plate and then chewing and swallowing it, with no enjoyment at all. Now, still chewing, she got up and began to clear the main course away. Eva scurried to help her.

'Don't bother,' said Mum. 'Go on talking to Dad.'

She was much more upset than Eva had realized. It was going to be difficult to get Dad to switch tracks in this mood. Eva went back to the table, peeled a banana and ate it slowly, enjoying every mouthful but waiting for a gap in the flow.

'Now, suppose you introduce into your group a mutation,' said Dad. 'Not anything physical, just some quirk, some trait, something like a slightly greater ability to intuit the causes of things, the why as well as the how . . .'

In the pause for breath Eva made her grunt and rattled out her question.

'Are they getting bananas at the Pool?'

'Bananas all round? Can't afford it. Where was I?'

'Hey! What about all these extra funds I'm earning for the benefit of the Pool?'

'They're for research and so on. I was saying . . .'

'Bananas are benefits if you're a chimp.'

'OK, when we're really rolling. But to go back . . .'

'You better take me up on Saturday. I'll do an opinion poll, find out how they want you to spend their funds. OK?'

You could use the box like that, pressing the keys while the other person was still talking. Somehow it forced even Dad to wait and see what you were going to say. He shrugged and gave up.

'I want to be with the others anyway,' said Eva.

'No,' said Mum.

She was standing in the doorway from the kitchen, looking as though someone had just died.

'No, darling,' she said again. 'I won't have it.'

Eva's hand froze over the keys.

'Now, listen, darling,' said Dad. 'What we think, Mum and I, is this . . .'

derstood. Mum didn't

learn about

find out things no one had known before. He probably still wanted that, but he wasn't prepared to fight for it, so he'd let Mum have her way for the time being, hoping that in a year or two Mum wouldn't mind so much; and in the meanwhile the whole business they'd just been talking about, giving her others like her, chimps with human minds . . . well they were going to do it anyway, but it was a sort of compromise, Dad's way of putting things, to keep everyone sort-of-happy . . .

Eva picked up her mug and slung it at the wall. It smashed. By then she was on the table, flailing the dishes onto the floor with a sweep of her arm. Mum screamed. Dad yelled at Eva to stop it. She ignored him and sprang across the room to the window, grabbed at the slats of the blind and ripped it down. Mum was shouting, 'No! Eva! No!' Dad was at his desk with his back to the room. He turned. He had a stun-gun in his hand, the sort they used at the Pool to lay out a chimp they couldn't handle any other way. As he raised it Eva snatched up a cushion and flung it at the gun, spoiling his aim. Before he could steady his arm she was on him. He tried to hang on but she was far too strong. She wrenched the gun from his fingers and backed off. Mum was crying. Eva faced Dad, panting.

Her whole body was still electric with the impulse to rush round the flat, breaking and destroying. She had watched the eruption almost as if from the outside, powerless to stop it, only able to direct it a little, using her human intelligence to recognize the gun, throw the cushion, snatch the weapon away. Now, with a big effort she forced herself to stand still and tap out a sentence. Deliberately she didn't press any of the tone codes.

'If you won't let me be a chimp there then I'll be a chimp here,' said the lifeless voice. Dad watched her, fright and fury in the set of his mouth, calculation in his eyes. He'd kept the gun ready and loaded, Eva thought. He'd known, really. She pointed it downwards and pressed the trigger. Phut, thud. The fine-needled dart quivered in the carpet. Mum stared at it, gulping to control her sobs. Eva pressed the keys again, but this time she coded in the human warmth.

'I'm sorry. It's there. It's part of me now. Please understand.'

Silence still.

'It doesn't mean I'll stop loving you.'

Dad turned and fiddled with the ruined blind, pretending he was trying to see whether it would mend. Eva put the gun on the desk and went and stood in front of Mum in the half-crouched position now natural to her, with one set of knuckles on the ground. She looked up into Mum's face. The blue eyes were blank, not stony and rejecting but empty, numb, lightless. Eva's whole instinct was to reach up and touch and caress, but she knew that would be a mistake. Mum managed an unhappy smile.

MONTH SIX, DAY TEN

A new life, a beginning . . .
Sun on a naked pelt . . .
Chimp odours, chimp voices . . .

Shivering with nerves, Eva waited. The rusty surface of a branch pressed its hard nodules into her soles. The iron trunk at her side was rougher and rustier still. In front of her rose a whole grove of iron trees, gaunt, leafless, five regular lines of them stretching away into the distance, rising from a barren grey floor whose pits and boulders had the same square, unnatural angles as the trees. Around the grove was a low cliff, with openings like the mouths of caves, only here again the square angles and straight edges showed that like everything else she could see the caves had been made by people.

Eva hadn't guessed she would find it so weird. She had seen it before, often, but with human eyes. Then the trees had been the iron pillars that had once supported the roof of a large factory, the boulders had been beds for heavy machinery, the surrounding caves had been offices and store-rooms. Beyond the roofless walls she could see the tops of the rest of the human forest, tower beyond tower, rising into the morning sky. The only reason that there were no towers here was that the ground below was riddled with the tunnels of an exhausted coal-mine, so in the old days the area had been used for industry. But then, Dad said, the tides of money had washed elsewhere and the area had gone derelict, just at the time when the last chimpanzees were being gathered out of the wild to form the Pool. Of course most of the people who'd done the agitating and signed the petitions had thought the chimps could come and live in a nice green park somewhere, like squirrels, but being chimps they'd have stripped the precious trees leafless in a couple of months. Instead they'd been put in this iron and concrete grove. It used to seem neat and convenient when Dad explained it, but it didn't now, not through chimp eyes. It seemed weird.

These ruined factories were the Reserve Section of the Pool. From here came the chimps in Dad's Research Section, and the ones who were sold to other scientists, and slightly luckier ones for people to go and look at in the cities. But this was their jungle, now, where as far as possible they were let be. Ropes

chimps could while human observers could still study most of what was going on from observation points up in the outer walls.

Dad was in one of these now, with Joey, the head keeper at the Reserve. They had a long-range stun-gun loaded and ready – Mum had insisted on that, and had made Eva promise she wouldn't go anywhere out of Joey's line of sight – but neither Eva nor Dad thought there'd be that sort of trouble. Chimp groups weren't like beehives or ants' nests, so close-knit that they'd kill a stranger who tried to join them. In the old jungle, Dad said, females had mostly stuck together in loose family networks – daughters, aunts, cousins – while the males had wandered around more. And nowadays the Pool was always swapping individuals from one section to another without any fuss, though sometimes it took them a day or two to fit in, and there were always a few who, like humans, were just plain unpopular. There was no reason why Eva shouldn't be OK, but still she was extremely nervous. She felt as though the next hour might be the most important in her whole new life.

She sniffed at the chimpy air and listened to the voices echoing among the iron trees – squabbles, happy-noises, the chitter-chatter of a baby pretending to be in trouble. The urge rose in her throat to answer, to cry her lonely-call, to make them come and find her. She controlled it. That wasn't how she wanted to start.

She'd been sitting in her tree for something like twenty minutes when a young adult male came rambling down past one of the machine-beds and saw her. She didn't know his name – she'd only known the chimps in the Research Section that well. She gave him the breathy hoot of greeting but he had something else on his mind and knuckled on out of sight. Still, the encounter calmed her nerves slightly – at least he'd seemed to think it was perfectly normal for this stranger to be sitting up there.

Another time passed by – she didn't know how long, she'd stopped thinking in minutes. Then a group of chimps emerged from one of the roofless rooms on the far side and came wandering towards where Eva sat. Three adult females and a four-year-old – Beth, Dinks, Lana, Buttons; Beth's son, Abel, one-and-a-half; Lana's baby, Wang. (The Pool staff took turns to name the chimps.) This was the group Eva had been waiting for. They usually made their way over here this time of the morning. She knew their names because Dad had shown her shapings of them last night.

Beth was elderly, grey around the ears, with a long, thin face; Dinks was an orphan who'd been sort-of-adopted by Beth a few years back when her own daughter had been sold for research; Buttons had been miserable in one of the public areas, so had been brought here and had just joined herself on to Beth's _____ niece. She was also Kelly's sis-_____winter, while

out actually _____
Eva had agreed they wouldn't ___

Either they didn't notice Eva sitting halfway up tree in 'their' patch, or they just ignored her. They came closer and closer. Her heart pounded. Her lips began to ripple with exploratory impulses of greeting

99

and beseeching. And then, frustratingly, they settled out of sight on the far side of a piece of wall that ran slantwise across the floor a few yards from Eva's perch. Perhaps, she realized, they *had* noticed her and didn't want to be watched by this stranger. She sat for a while, listening to the faint sounds they made. On the whole, unless they were having a squabble or one of them was frustrated in some way, chimps didn't 'talk' with their voices. Most of that sort of noise was used for calls – 'Danger!' 'Hurry!' 'Food!' Their language when they were resting peaceably was grimace and gesture and touch. Touch especially. All Eva could tell without seeing them was that one of them – probably Abel – was restless and being a nuisance, pestering the others to play. Nothing else happened, not here, though over on the far side of the space a real hullaballoo blew up between two males, and then died away.

After a while Eva climbed down from her tree, knuckled back towards the outer wall and picked up a plastic squash-bottle she'd noticed lying there. The staff deliberately dropped bits of harmless junk into the space to give the chimps objects to play with and use. On her way back she found a strip of coarse woven stuff. She hunkered down in the open just beyond the wall, about a dozen yards from Beth's group and began to unpick the cloth. The strands came out about two foot long. Slowly she tied them together. The knots were surprisingly difficult, not just because the chimp thumb is so short and awkward, but because her fingers didn't seem to understand what was expected of them. It was like tying knots in a dream. She managed to tie four strands into a length and then looped one end round the neck of the bottle and pulled it tight.

All this while she pretended to be absorbed in what she was doing, but she was aware that by now most of Beth's group had stopped reacting with each other and were watching her. Her spine prickled with their attention. Close in front of her there was a gap in the floor-level, some kind of sump or inspection-pit; it was dry, so it must drain away somewhere, but it had a jumble of rubbish in the bottom, old cabbage-stalks and peelings, bits of plastic, cans, cardboard. She dropped the bottle over the edge and backed away, holding the cord.

Her move took her beyond the edge of the wall, out of sight of the others. Hunkering down again she pulled on the cord, teasing the bottle up over the edge of the pit and then, slowly, across the floor towards her.

There was a scamper of feet – Abel, probably – and a bark – Beth calling him back. Eva whisked the bot-
_____ __ __ behind her back. Abel came
_____ Eva

bottle ac___
almost touched it, but as soon as ___
grab it Eva whisked it out of reach. She hid it and laughed again, then turned. Lana, she saw, was laughing too. A chimp's laugh is almost silent, a sucking of breath and a round toothless grin. Abel, suddenly

alarmed, went scuttering back to Beth. Beth rose slowly from where Dinks had been grooming her and came over. Her solid, deliberate movement showed she was boss of the group, and knew it, and expected this stranger to know it too. Eva crouched low and gave a series of brief, quiet pants – what Dad called 'submission-greeting', a way of saying You're the boss. Beth snorted, then lowered her head to within a few inches of Eva's and stared.

Eva couldn't stare back because that would have been a challenge; but flickering glances showed her there was something else in Beth's eyes than the assertion of dominance – puzzlement? Surprise? Eva was very aware now of her differences, of the people-smells she must carry, shampoo and cooking and trafficky streets, and inside her the human mind trying to control the encounter. She made more submission-pants and put out her left hand in a tentative pleading gesture. Beth backed away, still staring, but now with a frown of definite bewilderment. Almost as clear as speaking her look said, 'Where have I seen you before?'

Chimps had good memories, Eva knew. When she was five a young female called Snoo had been very fond of her and wanted to play with her all the time whenever Eva came. But then Snoo had gone off for a language experiment and Eva hadn't seen her for three whole years, so that Eva had changed a lot before they met again. Even so Snoo had known her at once and gone wild with excitement, jumping up and down and shrieking in her glee. So was it possible Beth actually remembered Kelly? Dad had said no. Chimps for the research section were taken away when they were still small, in order not to disrupt the community too much, so Kelly would have been less than a year old – tiny, when Beth had last seen her. It didn't seem possible. Still . . .

She tried the greeting again, but this time more confidently – not 'Good morning, Lady Elizabeth' but 'Hi, Mrs Beth.' Beth gave up the puzzle, whooshed her breath out and lumbered back to Dinks. Eva stayed where she was and made a loose loop in the end of her cord.

After a short while Abel came sidling across to look for the bottle. Eva rolled it towards him, then drew it back, coaxing him along till he was in reach. She picked the bottle up and teased him closer, then slipped the loop over his neck as she gave him the bottle. He grabbed and scampered away to play with his toy, not yet realizing it was fastened to him. After a while he took it to the pit and dropped it over the edge. Nothing happened, so he lost interest and moved off. As soon as the cord tightened he jerked away. The bottle shot into the open. Abel stared at it, _____ then backed off again. The bottle

until the _____
simply ran about, trailing the cord,
fun in that so he lost his temper and wrenched the cord off his neck.

The adults had watched his game intently, their heads moving to and fro as he scampered about.

When it was over Beth and Dinks went back to grooming but Lana turned towards Eva with a look of amusement crinkling round her eyes. They laughed together. Eva rose and lolloped across, then stopped. There was still, she sensed, an invisible barrier which it wasn't manners to go bursting through. Slowly she reached out with the same pleading gesture she had used towards Beth, but stretching further, further. Lana replied by pushing an arm towards her. Eva touched with her fingertips, walking them delicately up the flesh beneath the dark hairs, and then, when Lana didn't withdraw, hunkered down closer and began to groom her never-known sister in earnest.

It was some while before she realized that she had broken her promise by moving out of Joey's line of fire. By then she was sitting huddled close to Lana while Lana searched steadily down her shoulder blade and Wang scrambled his way over the pair of them, not seeming to notice which was which. Eva hadn't had a bath for four days, but she knew she must still smell strongly of the human world. Lana sniffed at her sometimes, inquisitively but not suspiciously. Sitting in the sun, being properly groomed by a real chimp who did it because she wanted to and not just because she was supposed to was the most glorious sensation. Eva had never felt closer to anyone. The only trouble was that Lana wasn't going to find any reward for her search. She didn't seem to mind, but Eva had picked off and nibbled half a dozen little bugs that had moved in under Lana's fur.

I must get me some bugs of my own, she thought. Mum's not going to like that.

*

104

'How did you get on, darling?'

'OK. Bit like first day at school. I think some of them sort of guessed I was funny, but then they forgot.'

Mum had tried to make her question casual but you could hear the edge in it. Eva, on the other hand, could control her tone exactly, using the box. It wasn't fair, but it couldn't be helped.

'I'm going to find lots out for Dad,' she said.

'Good.'

Not fair, either. Eva was preparing Mum to accept that she was going back to the Pool as often as she could. At the same time she was concealing the row she'd had with Dad, first because of moving out of sight and then by losing all track of time, so that in order to attract her attention he'd had to break the Reserve rule of not making the chimps aware of the human presence more than he had to. Still, she was fairly certain he wouldn't tell Mum. He was too excited about the new project of having Eva see if she

graphs and seeing

friend but you haven't thought about for years. I *must* write her a card, you tell yourself, and perhaps you do, but that's all.

Eva pressed the keys again, coding in pleasure and excitement.

'I made a friend,' she said.

'That's nice,' said Mum automatically, but stopped her next sentence before she'd begun it. Why don't you ask her round? it would have been, but that didn't make sense now.

Living two lives . . .
Yesterday the Reserve, the silent iron trees, the sun-
*   light . . .*
Friendly fingers creeping across a shoulder blade . . .
Peace . . .
Today clamour, scurry, pressure . . .
Today people . . .

Bobo snatched off Jenny's spectacles and bit them in
two. One of Mr Coulis's helpers tried to grab him,
but he flung her away, snarling. Mr Coulis himself
came hurrying, but stopped when Bobo lurched at
him with his hair bushed out under his cowboy shirt

guard-rail the whole tower rattled and quivered and
two loose lights fell off, their bulbs exploding when
they hit the ground. The noise excited him further.
Everyone was yelling now. Mr Coulis had started to
climb the ladder but Bobo saw him coming and slung

a screwdriver at him, hitting him on the cheek. He scrambled down with blood beginning to stream on to his shirt. Bobo tried to wrench a fixed light off the rail.

Mimi began to screech. She was a shaper-director, quite well-known for her pictures and even better-known for her extravagance and tantrums. She was a short, square, yellow-faced woman who always wore red-and-black outfits with chunky necklaces and bangles. In a tantrum she threw her arms about, so that the bangles clashed, out of key with her screeches. Mr Coulis tried to placate her with little bobs and shrugs while he dabbed at his cheek with a bloody handkerchief. It wasn't his fault. The script had called for a *big* chimp, and that meant a male. Bobo hadn't done ads before, but he'd always been fairly easy-going and less unpredictable than the other males. And so on. Mimi paid no attention.

The four trained chimps – Jenny, Belinda, Olo, Nin – watched both exhibitions with wariness. They probably found the human row more frightening. To see a male chimp in a rage was an everyday thing for them, but to see humans making the same kind of noises, giving the same kind of signals, especially to Mr Coulis, whom they'd been trained to regard as dominant – that was new and alarming. Humans had immense and magical powers. What mightn't one of *them* do in a tantrum?

Eva also watched, but with increasing exasperation. She hated these ad-sessions anyway, but it was in the contract so she had to do them. In a minute or two Mr Coulis would have to lay Bobo out with his stun-gun, and that would mean no more filming

108

today and trying again tomorrow. Tomorrow she wanted to go back to the Reserve. After that it would be at least two weeks before she got another chance to spend time with Lana, to sit in the sun and groom and be groomed and watch Wang learning the rules of the concrete grove. Eva's diary was full for three days after tomorrow, and then for the next ten she'd be in oestrus. This happened once every thirty-five days – your sex-parts on your rump swelled up and became tender and the males got excited about you. There were pills Eva could have used to suppress it but they made her feel sick and low. Being in oestrus didn't bother Eva herself much – far less than she'd expected – and the males at the Reserve wouldn't have done anything unless she'd let them, but they'd have hung around and begged, and she'd have felt she was making a difference between herself and the other females by shooing them off – and anyway, Mum wouldn't have dreamed of letting her go to the Reserve like that. By the time oestrus was over it

the chance. But there was Mr Coulis here, and all these other humans, and besides he'd lived most of his life in Research, and now in a Public Area, both of which were even less natural than the Reserve. He didn't know where to begin. His solution was the usual male one – he threw a tantrum.

'I'm on the big fellow's side, myself,' said a man's voice close by.

'I don't care. I want my tea-break,' said a woman.

Eva sat by herself between takes, not just because there was a chair marked 'Eva', but because anything else was impossible. She was too conscious of her difference from the other chimps to stay with them – in this world they were chimps but she was people – but she didn't feel like talking to people either. Her only thought was to get the whole thing over and go away. Now she merely glanced sideways and saw the couple, a pretty woman with a bored face and a plump young man with a pale gold beard. He noticed Eva's glance and smiled.

'How about you, miss?' he said.

Eva grunted, a no-meaning sound.

'It's just against reason and nature,' said the man, still speaking to Eva. 'Bringing a noble beast like that into this kind of crappy set-up and getting him to do anything we fancy, such as being kitted up for laughs in a cowboy outfit. It makes me sick.'

'It's a living,' said the woman.

'God, now look! They're going to lay him out!' said the man.

Mr Coulis was checking the stun-gun over. Exasperation flooded through Eva. In a couple of seconds she'd have been up among the lights, screeching and throwing like Bobo but she just managed to control her fury. She picked up her keyboard from the floor beside her and tapped out a sentence.

'Tell them to turn the lights off.'

The man nodded and turned away. Eva handed the keyboard to the woman and knuckled across the floor to where Mr Coulis was raising the stun-gun to take aim. He didn't see her coming until she reached up and pulled the muzzle down. He looked at her, astonished. She shook her head like a human and held up her free hand, palm forward, in a signal for him to wait.

Bobo, sensing that he was losing his audience's attention, began jumping up and down, making his tower clatter to his rhythm.

Then the main lights went out. Though there were still a few ordinary house-lights burning the effect was like sudden dusk, a forest dark, especially up above among the looped and trailing cables. Bobo was startled into silence. Everyone waited.

Eva knuckled across to the group of females and faced them. They were all, of course, young, used to being bossed by adults and also by humans. They were frightened, too, grinning and showing their

Eva wanted. They

females in the public section ganging up, three or four together, to counteract the bullying of one of the males.

Eva turned, still holding Belinda's wrist but using her free arm to knuckle across to the tower. Belinda didn't resist. At the foot of the tower Eva let go and began to climb. When she reached the first strut she stopped and looked down. Belinda was hesitating, one hand on an upright, but the other three were now moving, half hypnotized, to join her. Eva beckoned encouragingly and climbed on. Above her Bobo had stopped his jumping and had begun to screech. The whole studio rang with the racket, but Eva knew it wasn't as terrifying as it sounded to human ears. To the chimps it meant something different – Bobo himself was scared. Strong as he was he couldn't cope with five females if they chose to attack him.

She swung herself across to the far side of the tower and swarmed rapidly up, coming out on the platform behind Bobo, who was still watching her allies climbing the side of the tower that faced out into the studio. She knuckled across, reached up and touched him on the shoulder. He jumped several inches and spun round, his face one enormous grin with his big emergent canines gleaming in the gloom.

Eva, the moment she'd touched him, had backed off, crouched down and begun the quick pants of submission. Bobo stared, baffled. He didn't notice the heads of the allies appearing over the rim of the platform. They too stared for a moment, then hesitatingly swung themselves on to the platform and gave Bobo the same signal Eva was giving. Olo presented him her rump, but as she was wearing jeans this didn't have any effect.

Bobo sat down. His grin was still huge, but his teeth were hardly showing at all now. Eva immediately crouched beside him and started grooming attentively through the fur of his neck. Nin joined on the other side, and the remaining three settled into a huddle to groom each other. The humans muttered below, a gentle, almost pleasing sound. Then the whole group tensed as someone started to climb the ladder. Bobo stirred apprehensively, though Eva did her best to calm him with comforting little clicks. As soon as Mr Coulis's face appeared above the edge of the platform she held up her hand towards him, fingers spread. Five minutes. The face ducked out of sight.

Jenny and Olo swung themselves across and peered over to watch Mr Coulis going down the ladder. When they came back they looked at Eva for several seconds, and then Olo settled beside her and began to search through her nape-hairs. Bobo turned, put his arm round her, and gave her the big, open-mouthed chimp kiss. He did it without thinking, of course. It was what he wanted to do. He'd always been a naturally gentle and affectionate chimp.

the humans down too, and stopped their screeching, made the mad world sensible for a little, and known the signal to send the dominant human back down the ladder. When eventually she rose and beckoned to them to follow they all climbed down without fuss.

Somebody had had the sense to produce a bunch of bananas. Eva tore it in two, gave half to Bobo and shared the rest among her allies.

As soon as the first take was over – of course it didn't go smoothly because nothing with chimps and nothing with shaper people ever did – Mr Coulis took his chimps off out of sight to a large cage where they could be alone. Eva went back to her chair at the edge of the studio. The woman had gone, but the young man with the beard was waiting with her keyboard.

'That worked out pretty damn well,' he said. 'First time in years I've seen my mother upstaged.'

'Uh?'

'Yeah. I don't belong. I'm Mimi Venturi's son. We got into an argument about whether she should have taken this assignment on. You know how it happened? Honeybear were all set to stop using chimps in their ads and go in for swanky-arty, so they hired my mother. Then you showed up and they decided to stick with the chimps. They wanted to back out of their contract but my mother needed the money, so they said OK, but in that case you've got to direct the chimps. My mother says chimps are hell, but they're less hell than actors, and anyway who am I to tell her she's wasting her talents. I say the hell with your talents, you're wasting chimps. She says they love it. I say crap. She says come and see. Now I've seen.'

'They like it when people give them fruit. Otherwise, no.'

'I'll tell her.'

'I hate it all, but the Pool needs the money.'

'Same the whole world over.'

'At least I can go home after. What's your name?'

114

'Call me Grog. It's short for Giorgio. Grog Kennedy, because my mother was married to a guy of that name when I got born. She's had eight husbands but I wasn't any of theirs. I guess if you looked in the history books you could find there've been worse mothers, but I haven't met any.'

He sounded perfectly cheerful about it. In fact it didn't sound as if he minded anything much. You'd have taken him for a very relaxed, easy-going, pleasant young man, if it hadn't been for the vehemence, the passion, which Eva had heard in his voice when he'd been talking to the woman about Bobo's outburst. Eva liked him, in a way which she didn't often experience nowadays with new people. There was nothing in anything he said, in tone or glance or gesture, which suggested that he didn't find it perfectly normal to be talking to her. Even Bren (even Mum, still) couldn't do that, quite.

'What do you think ought to happen to us?' she said.

Uh?

'Sure. Haven't you noticed? We're opting out, not trying any more, living in the past. We conquered the planet, and what has it done for us? Zilch. All we've got is one ruined planet. How long d'you think we're going to go on looking after a bunch of monkeys? I

115

tell you, Eva, you better be thinking, and thinking now, how you chimps are going to start getting a living for yourselves without us.'

He actually meant it. Eva could hear. Though his voice stayed light and level the passion was back. Eva hadn't meant to talk at all, and even now didn't feel like getting into a proper conversation. She could have explained about the several attempts there'd been in the old days to teach chimps from zoos and research establishments how to live wild and look after themselves, and how difficult it had been, though a few of them had managed it; but tapping out all that stuff would have taken so long, and besides she wasn't sure of the details. Grog sounded the kind of nutter who needed chapter and verse before he would accept anything.

'You better come round and talk to Dad,' she said. 'He's read all the books.'

'Like to meet him. Sure that's OK?'

Eva grunted and told him the number to call. He wrote it down, then squatted cross-legged on the floor beside her. He seemed to understand her mood, and dropped back into his amused, detached voice, telling her all about himself in a way which meant she could keep the talk going with just a grunt here and there. He was twenty-seven, older than he looked. He didn't have a job because, he said, Mimi bust up anything he started on; she liked to have him around, he said, as a way of getting her revenge on men. Marrying them was another way. In spite of what he said Eva guessed he was actually rather fond of his mother, but having to cope with her meant that he didn't have any spare emotions to spend on

116

other people. Instead, his love, his passion, came out in his feeling for animals. He wasn't very realistic about it because he hadn't had much chance to learn what animals are actually like, but judging by the way he dealt with her Eva felt he'd pick up anything he needed very quickly. Without thinking what she was doing she started to groom her way up through the short gold hairs at the corner of his jaw. He accepted her touch without comment, simply adjusting his position so that she could work more easily.

The chimps came back for the next take in a jumpy mood, but as soon as Eva knuckled down to meet them they crowded round her, panting and touching. Even Bobo half forgot his dignity and tried to greet her as though she'd been boss. They needed the reassurance of her presence, the understanding that nothing unpredictable or ugly would happen to them while she was around. Very much to her surprise Eva found that she actually enjoyed the sense of power

and snarl at Jenny,

and behave. Bobo himself as the day went on became more and more fretful, but the others understood the importance of keeping him happy. Belinda half accidentally organized a sort of rota so that Bobo always had a couple of females paying attention to him. By the end of the day Belinda was also trying to copy some of the grunts and gestures which she'd seen Eva using to control the threatening swarm of humans.

The whole thing ended with the shoot-out. It was mostly done by tricks and cameras. Bobo had a gun taped to his hand, and of course he just waved it about and tried to shake it free and pull it off, but by piecing tiny bits of that together they were going to make it look as if he'd drawn it from his holster. Eva's gun was a trick banana. She drew it and pulled the trigger; the skin split open and the banana shot across the saloon, finishing in Bobo's mouth (more tricks). It all ended with him sitting down and munching away, which he happened actually to do first go, with exactly the right look of having decided he was tired of being a baddie and was now going to become a model citizen. Pure accident, of course, but all the humans laughed and cheered, as much with the relief of having got the assignment over as with real amusement. The studio echoed with their baying cackle. Coming from a Public Area with humans gawping at them all day long, Mr Coulis's chimps were used to the noise and paid no attention, but Eva felt her whole skin prickle with fright and rage. The urge to get clear was overpowering. She saw a couple of studio assistants coming her way, their kids' autograph books open and ready. Normally she'd have done what they wanted, but today she swung away and scampered across to where she'd left her keyboard by her chair. Grog was still standing there, staring at the scene with a look of real hatred.

'Don't forget,' she said. 'Call Dad.'

'Will do.'

She grunted and knuckled away to her dressing room.

MONTH EIGHT, DAYS FOUR AND SIX

Living – just living.
What for?
The apes in the iron grove, waiting, purposeless ...
The people cramming the pavements, cramming the
    travellers, their faces all fret, purposeless ...
Eva, between ...
What for?

Grog hit it off a dream with Mum – with Dad, too, in a different way. He even managed it with both together. When he had Dad to himself he let Dad do all the talking, just asking the odd question to nudge the conversation on. At the same time, Eva noticed, he gave Dad little signals of deference while still managing to seem quite free and independent. With Mum he talked gossip, mostly. Tagging along with Mimi he'd met shaper-stars, artists, billionaires, and they fell naturally into the talk. He had a story about them, or knew what they were really like, and told her. If Dad had been listening he'd have felt a need to compete with famous people *he'd* met, and then got huffy because they weren't as famous as Grog's. And Grog listened. He remembered what Mum told him – the names and doings of people she tried to help in her job, and he laughed or sympathized with their stories, and so on. It seemed perfectly genuine. Eva decided he was just interested in people, in his rather detached way, because they were people, not because they were famous. She said so one day and he shook his head.

'Sure, I'm interested,' he said. 'What you mean is I'm not impressed – just like I'm not impressed by money. I'm interested though, because money's useful. How's old Beth doing?'

Eva gave him the chimp-gossip – he was interested in that too. Only later did she wonder whether he'd brought Beth up so as to stop her asking what he was going to use his famous friends for – he didn't need anything, or seem to want anything. She began to watch him with different eyes, noticing, for instance, how when he had Mum and Dad together he would usually side with Mum in an argument, somehow without actually contradicting Dad, and how in these arguments if they had anything to do with chimps or conservation Grog seemed better informed each time he came. He must have been reading a lot and watch-

ty well ill. They

out, so she hid on a wide shelf above some rubbish bins which were housed in a shed by the car park. The bricks had gaps between them so that the air stayed fresh round the bins, which allowed Eva to watch the entrance for Mum's car. Eva had never really taken the idea that anyone would want to kidnap her seriously, but Dad did, and Honeybear had put it into the contract that she had to have a bodyguard, so there was a good chance Cormac would have got the sack if she'd been spotted hanging around alone.

At first she just crouched there, enjoying her peace and privacy, easing herself into the transition between her two lives. Time went by and she began to feel anxious. She could feel her lips tensing and drawing back to show her teeth. Then she heard a familiar voice. 'Saturday again, OK?' 'Far as I know, Grog.' 'Right, so long.' He strolled past only a few yards away. She was off the shelf and scampering after him before she had time to wonder why he was there. He turned at the sound of her feet and smiled.

'Hi, Eva. Thought you'd gone home.'

'Mum's taken Cormac to the dentist. She's late.'

'Uh huh. Had a good time?'

He hadn't seemed even faintly surprised or put out to see her, but now there was something in his tone, in the quickness of the question, trying to put the talk on to ground of his own choosing, which stopped her answering normally. She grunted an OK and changed the subject.

'Why are you here?'

'Just interested.'

'Does Dad know?'

People had to get special permission, with good reasons, to come to the Reserve. The Public Section was for the gawpers.

'Guess not. Didn't want to bother him.'

122

Her grunt this time was surprise and doubt, but at that moment Mum drove into the car park.

'No time now,' he said. 'Don't worry – it's all in a good cause. Tell you about it – uh, when's the next commercial?'

'Day after tomorrow.'

'OK, I'll drive you to the studios. Pick you up half-past eight. Tell you on the way. Hi, Lil, good to see you.'

'What on earth are you doing up here?'

'Making a date with your daughter.'

As usual he managed it perfectly – teasing, a bit mysterious, making her understand she'd just get teased again if she went on, so that she'd better shut up.

'Thursday, then,' he said. 'Eight-thirty, sharp. Hi, Cormac. See you, Lil.'

He strolled away.

'What was that about?' said Mum.

'Don't know – only he's taking me to the studios so ⋯plain why he's been nosing around. How's ⋯mac?'

⋯ small and old and ⋯he fact that he ⋯job and

⋯
side-rou⋯
want to talk, so ⋯

'What were you doing⋯'

'Watching. Learning.'

'Why?'

'Tell you when we get there. There'll be time.'

As he spoke his head moved fractionally. To Cormac, crouching enormous on the back seat, it probably looked just the result of a jolt, but Eva understood. They reached their destination with a good half-hour to spare.

Honeybear rented a studio from one of the big shaper companies, and the car they sent for Eva used to drive round to that wing, but Grog pulled up in front of the soaring transmission tower.

'Slot one-two-oh-eight in the parking block,' he said. 'Take her round for me, will you, Cormac? See you in the studio. Thanks.'

At the main entrance he showed a pass to the security guard who said 'Hi, Grog, nice morning . . . hey, is this Eva?' Eva shook the guard's hand and followed Grog through the huge hallway to the lifts. At the hundred-and-somethingth floor the lift voice said, 'Terminus. Terminus. Upper floors not yet open.' Grog slid a plastic card into a slot and the lift went on up.

'OK,' he said as it slowed. 'I want to carry you this bit. Shut your eyes. Don't open them till I say or you'll spoil the fun. Huh! You're heavier than I guessed!'

Mystified, Eva closed her eyes and clung. She heard the doors open and smelt food-smells. Grog's footsteps made no noise on a thick carpet. He stopped and she heard the faint flip of switches, then the hum of a shaper zone warming – more than one, and huge, making her fur creep with static. The hum died as the zones settled into their shapes.

'OK, you can look now,' said Grog.

124

She opened her eyes and saw jungle – dark, rich greenness, swaying faintly. Now the noises began, rustles, bird-calls, a weird distant howling, the splash of water. But no smells, only yesterday's food. An enormous orange spider scuttled across the brown dead leaves towards Grog's feet, and vanished. It wasn't real. It had just reached the edge of the zone. She turned her head and over Grog's shoulder saw a table and chairs, and a little way off another one in another gap in the zones; then another and another; and then, further off still, daylight, the brilliant sky over the city, seen through big windows high up in the tower.

'Uh?' she grunted.

'Executive Restaurant,' said Grog. 'Centre of the world, kind of. The fat bastards who decide what we're all going to see and think sit in their offices and look at the instant feedback figures and then they come up here and fight it out over their steaks what we're going to see and think next. They can't do a

with blue green waves breaking into surf. He brought the jungle back.

'It's not even tape,' he said. 'It's real. This very minute, out in Cayamoro, that snake's looking for tree frogs.'

The snake was pale green, with a dark stripe along

its spine. Eva felt herself shudder at the sight of it. She almost jumped back into Grog's arms. She hadn't minded snakes when she'd been human – not on the shaper, anyway. Now it was Kelly's impulse, barely controllable, to leap away and chatter her fright. Teeth bared, she watched the snake slide out of sight. It took her a minute or two more to gather the courage to explore.

Of course Eva had seen jungle on the shaper at home, but there the zone only filled a bit of the living room, less than life-size. You could walk into it, but it was all so crowded that you couldn't help walking through the shapes, and you felt huge, and you could see out all round to the same old walls and chairs and pictures. This was different. It was almost real, apart from the tables and chairs. Faint marks on the floor showed the narrow pathways between the zones where the guests and the waiters came and went, but on either side you seemed to peer deep into living jungle, succulent leaves, shaggy peeling bark which might have fat grubs underneath, trailing strands of creeper jewelled with yellow berries. A humming-bird darted across a space, its wings a blur, emerald mist. Beneath the leaf-litter something moved, emerged, jet black, a millipede eight inches long. Between two trunks stretched a strange white vague thing; small orange spiders scuttled through it, hundreds of them; it was their communal web; when a moth blundered into it they were on their victim in a flash. All around was a sense of danger. Could you eat the berries, the bugs, the leaves? Was the millipede deadly? Or the snake?

But along with the danger was excitement, yearning.

This was where you belonged. This was Kelly's dream.

Eventually she knuckled her way back and found Grog standing by one of the wide windows, staring south.

'Uh?' she said.

'Going to see the real thing,' he said. 'I'm flying out to Cayamoro, day after tomorrow.'

'Uh?'

'Just have a look round. Size things up. People too.'

You couldn't just go to Cayamoro like that. But Grog could. He held up a finger.

'Hear that?' he said.

The far faint wail had begun again.

'Howler monkey,' he said. 'Jungle should be full of that noise, but they got their sums wrong when they set it all up. The howler population's gone down and down. They're not going to survive. So there's room for a new big ape in Cayamoro.'

Eva understood at once what he was talking about.

to remember he's got a whole lot of his life tied up in the Pool. One thing I've learnt is we're going to have a tougher time educating humans than we are educating chimps.'

'It's been tried.'

'Sure – I've read the literature, Stella Brewer, for instance, great girl, trying to teach chimps how to live in the wild after they'd been used for learning experiments, lived in houses, worn clothes, eaten off plates.'

'I thought some of hers were wild.'

'Yeah. Brought in as babies by poachers, and some of them she won with too – just a few. None of that matters. All I know is we've got to try again. We can't go on as we are. You've been born with the Pool, Eva, grown up with it. It's an always-there thing for you. But it isn't. The way things are going, in twenty years' time the Pool will be finished.'

'Uh!'

'I've seen the figures. To you being short of funds is just another always-there thing, but it's been getting worse. There's a trend. It started long before you were born. I'm not just talking about the Pool and I'm not just talking about money. It's happening all over. The whole human race is thinking in shorter and shorter terms. The bright kids aren't going into research, the investors aren't putting their money into anything that doesn't give them a quick return, governments and institutions aren't funding basic research, we're pulling back from space exploration, you name it, we're not doing it. We're giving up. Packing in.'

'Uh?'

'Trouble with us humans is we keep forgetting we're animals. You know what happens when an animal population expands beyond what the set-up will bear? Nature finds ways of cutting them back. Usually it's plain starvation, but even when there's food to go round something gets triggered inside them. They stop breeding, or they eat their own babies or peck each other to death – there's all sorts of ways. Us too. It's in us. We can't escape it. A lot of it's been going on already for years without anyone noticing, a sort of retreat, a backing-out, nine-tenths of the world's population holed up in their apartments twenty-four hours a day watching the shaper. But it's starting to move now. I can feel it. There's a real crash coming, and us being humans, whatever it is, we're going to overdo it. You know what that means for you chimps? Lana's children, or her children's children, are going to have to fend for themselves. You think they'll make it out there?'

He flicked his head towards the endless vista of towers, veiled in their human haze.

'Not a hope,' he said. 'They've got to be somewhere where there's trees to shelter them, leaves that come and come, fruit all the year round, small game

couldn't lead, they could only push – push the chimps out into a world where humans didn't fit. It makes your heart bleed, how they tried, the things they gave up. But you could lead, Eva.'

'Uh!'

'You and the others. Stefan's due to wake up, any day now.'

'Uh?'

'Chimp used to be called Caesar. Yasha's a month behind. Then there'll be three of you.'

Eva had not asked about Caesar since the night of her tantrum, and Mum and Dad hadn't mentioned him either, though Mum was probably hoping that when Joan's other patients began to wake, to become available for company, then Eva would stop wanting to spend so much time at the Reserve. Eva wasn't sure what she felt about this. Some ways it would be good to know chimps who could also talk – bitch about friends, discuss music, tease, plan lives – but she had now discovered other kinds of talk, in glance and gesture and especially touch, which gave her everything she needed.

'What do you think you're *for*?' said Grog.

'Uh?'

'Yeah. What are you *for*, Eva? What's your purpose? Are you just a freak? Are you just here so Professor Pradesh can prove things about neurone memory? Course, that's why the old girl chimped you, but do you reckon it's enough? Are you happy with just that? Being a scientific curiosity and selling drinks on the shaper? Listen. Your dad and the people who helped chimp you all did it for their own reasons, and your mum said yes to save your life. They didn't know the real reason. The real reason was that you and Stefan and the others are the ones who are going to show the chimps how to survive. Nature doesn't like letting species go. She's going to save the chimps if she can, and that's why she let you happen.'

Eva stared. She would hardly have known him. He stood in the brilliant morning light with the shaper jungle behind him, hunched, pop-eyed, quivering with the energies of his argument. She fluttered her fingers across the keys to tell him he was crazy. His whole idea was doubly impossible. You couldn't teach chimps to live on their own, not any longer. You couldn't persuade people to let you try. But try to tell Grog that. He simply wouldn't understand. He was like his mother in one of her rages, an unstoppable force, blind with his passion. She cancelled the words and just grunted doubt.

'Yeah,' he said. 'It'll take a bit of thinking about. Don't expect you to give me a yes right off. It's a long-term project – five years minimum. We've got to make a whole world see reason. They will in the end – they've got no other choice. But for you, Eva, do you want this . . .'

He waved a hand at the green compelling jungle.

'. . . or this?'

for guests who would never come.

'Time to go,' said Grog. 'Got to keep in with my mother – we're going to need her.'

MONTH EIGHT,
DAY TWENTY-NINE

Living with the dream . . .
Imaginary trees filling the iron grove . . .
Shadows, leaf-litter, looping creepers, the flash of a
  bird . . .
Calls, whispers, odours . . .

A card had come from Grog that morning, saying he
was staying a week longer because he'd picked up
some kind of jungle bug, but the picture of Cayamoro
was more beautiful than anything she'd ever seen. So,
now, as she played with Abel she did so absent-
mindedly, making imaginary scenarios of escape, not
just herself but Lana and Beth and the rest of them –
putting something in their food that would send them
all to sleep, and flying them south and then letting
them wake, amazed, among the odours and shadows
they were made for . . .

A shriek! Lana! Another! Eva scuttled round the
corner of the concrete slab against which she'd been
leaning. Lana was lying flat on her face on the ground
with a male chimp jumping on her. Beth and Dinks
were watching, shrieking too, with all their teeth
showing, outraged but too scared to help. Wang was
actually under Lana, squealing each time the weight
of the male came down. The male had his back to

Tatters was challenging him. Tatters would have won a straight fight easily enough, but Geronimo had the females on his side. Beth, in particular, supported him, partly because she was used to him, but partly because having the boss on her side helped her to dominate the younger females. Geronimo made a point of going round the female sub-groups and sitting grooming with each of them. Tatters's latest movie in the contest was trying to break this alliance up by attacking any females who paid attention to Geronimo. Presumably he'd seen Lana and Geronimo grooming, before Eva had arrived that morning, so he'd tried to punish her. He hadn't seriously hurt her. There were rules. Males never used their terrifying teeth to bite females, though they did sometimes with other males. He might possibly have killed Wang, but that would have been an accident. Certainly he wouldn't have expected a surprise ambush by a single female – that wasn't in the rules. If he worked out what had happened, Eva guessed, she'd be in for a rough time.

Now, attracted by the uproar, Geronimo came rambling over, with a young male called Sniff who tended to follow Geronimo around. Geronimo settled on to a slab with his back towards the tree. As soon as Beth noticed him she came over and greeted him with quick submissive bows and pants. He looked round in a lordly way and pretended to notice Tatters in the tree for the first time. Beth settled beside him and began to groom him. Dinks came over and presented her rump to him and then joined in grooming the other side. The three females left at the foot of the tree didn't feel confident enough to go on shrieking at

Tatters without the support of Beth and Dinks, so they backed off and settled down together. Eva put her arm round Lana to comfort her for her bad treatment, while Lana began to inspect Wang for signs of damage. Wang was trembling with fright, and stared at the world with shining, baffled eyes.

There would be cameras running up in the observation posts, and students taking notes, but they were all outside the story. Eva was inside it. She could feel little Wang's fright and Lana's quick recovery to her usual contented self. She could feel too that Lana hadn't seen how she'd been rescued. When Geronimo slowly turned to look up at Tatters, still grinning in the iron tree, and raised a beckoning hand to him inviting him down, Eva could sense both the mockery in the gesture and the genuine suggestion of peace-making. Tatters stayed where he was. His teeth still gleamed inside his tight-drawn lips, showing he was worried and nervous, though the threat from the females had gone. Perhaps, Eva thought, he was

being watched, by Sniff. He was

yards off, with his head bowed as if lost in some private dream, but his eyes were darting from side to side. The moment Eva caught his glance he looked away. This happened two or three times, until she realized that Sniff was actually doing much the same

135

that she was, watching deliberately in order to learn how things worked. The moment he realized that she'd been staring at him he turned his back on her.

The wild thought struck her that Sniff was actually like her, another chimp with a human mind, whom Dad hadn't told her about. No, impossible. Everything that had happened from her first waking, right through to the things people said during her check-ups in Joan's lab, made her certain she was the only one. So far.

At last Tatters came down from the tree and ambled off. Lana was feeling very possessive about Wang, and Dinks and Beth were still busy with Geronimo, but Abel, who'd been frightened enough by the fight to go and nestle against Beth's side, became restless again, so Eva took him off to continue their game. This consisted on a variation of the original trick with the bottle and cord, which allowed Eva sometimes to tie him a loose knot and when it came undone to see if he could be persuaded to try and re-tie it himself. At first he'd just held the ends together and hoped, and then brought it to Eva to mend, but she had refused to re-tie the knot unless he sat and watched what she was doing. Now, when it came apart, he'd got as far as twisting the ends together before giving up – anything like a real knot was still an accident.

They were sitting together, Eva knotting the loose ends with clear exaggerated movements, and Abel peering with his nose so close to her fingers that it looked as if he was trying to understand the process by smell, when she felt a faint movement against her shoulder. She looked round and saw Sniff crouching just behind her, watching what she was doing. He backed away at once, but she turned and gave him a quick pant of greeting, then finished tying the knot and gave the toy to Abel, who scampered away, trailing it behind him.

Sniff sat gazing at her. He was a slightly odd-looking chimp with a shorter, squarer face than most and very large pale ears. He wasn't quite full-grown, but Eva had the impression that even when he was he still wouldn't be as big as Tatters or Geronimo. He faced her with a bright, steady stare, challenging and inquisitive. She was aware at once that he had realized she was different. He wanted to know why.

This was new to Eva. Most of the chimps she'd met probably vaguely realized there was something a bit odd about her, but didn't distinguish Eva's kind of oddity from the oddities of some of the other chimps – Lulu's deafness or Gran's refusal to mate, ever. She panted again and moved up beside him, but when she started to groom him he took her hand in his and ...... before letting go.

staring at it when a ....

the slab. Together they rose and peered over the top.

Tatters had come back. Eva could see the back of his head and shoulders with his hair all bushed out as he swayed and stamped to and fro, hooting softly. Beth and Dinks, out of sight, were shrieking at him.

137

Eva knuckled round to the corner of the slab to watch the whole scene. Geronimo had actually turned his back on Tatters, trying to pretend he wasn't there, but Beth and Dinks had stopped grooming to watch Tatters and shriek. Tatters was an alarming sight. With his hair bushed out and his ponderous stamping movements he managed to make himself look even larger and heavier than he really was. The rhythm of his stamping increased. Dinks noticed Eva and held out a beseeching hand – 'Come and help'. Eva turned her head to look for Lana, who was out of sight, so she started forward to join the others but before she reached them Tatters charged, not directly at Geronimo but between him and Beth, knocking them both over. He swung his charge into a circling move-ment and finding Eva directly in his path he slapped her aside, sending her head over heels. She screeched and rose with her head ringing. The slap had been a terrific buffet, but it hadn't actually hurt all that much. Still, it was an outrage. Geronimo was on his feet now, screeching too, a little uncertainly, but with Beth and Dinks beside him he gathered the courage to rush at Tatters. Lana had appeared from somewhere and joined in, so Eva did too. Together they drove Tatters up the tree again. Sniff, Eva noticed, did noth-ing, but watched the whole episode from a few yards off.

Twenty minutes later, at Geronimo's invitation, Tatters came down and this time the two males set-tled down to an intensive grooming session, totally absorbed, locked into each other's arms. This was perfectly ordinary. It was the way most fights ended. It was even ordinary that a little later when Eva had started her game with Abel again, Beth came ambling past and seemed to notice her. She stared a moment, puzzled, and then without warning rushed at Eva and bit her hard on the shoulder. Eva shrieked – the bite hurt a good deal more than the buffet from Tatters. Abel raced off. Lana came over, beginning to shriek too, but instead of continuing the fight Beth knuckled rapidly away, leaving Lana to comfort Eva and lick the bite-mark, which had actually drawn blood. Eva sat trembling with shock, but she knew she shouldn't have been surprised. Beth must have seen the attack on Tatters and known what had happened, and though she had joined in driving Tatters up the tree she still couldn't approve of a junior female acting with that kind of initiative. So as soon as she'd recovered from her shakes, Eva went and found Beth and gave her a very formal submissive bow and pant, just to keep things straight. Beth, of course, pretended not to notice but was clearly pleased. This was something Eva could see and feel but the researchers in the

tion grille in it and a lock humans chimps couldn't – a box with a tricky catch and inside it a four-digit code to punch. Eva had slipped through and was putting on her overalls when she heard a movement and glanced up. Four chimp fingers were gripped into the grille. Quickly Eva switched the light

MONTH NINE, DAY FOURTEEN

Living in the real world . . .
No dreams, only people.
Rush and crush.
Winter again, soon.

Eva made a tape to take to Grog in hospital. On one
side she put the reasons why she wasn't going to help
him in his campaign to get the chimps moved to
Cayamoro. Long arguments like that she usually put
on tape, because it took such ages to spell them out,
face to face. She had plenty of reasons – reasons to do
with chimps. (How could you loose chimps in wild
jungle when they didn't know a poisonous berry from

people who looked after Cayamoro

lot of chimps in their jungle? And so on.) Eva's own
reasons . . .

She found these harder to get said but she had to,
to be fair on Grog. She was happy with things as they
were. Perhaps 'happy' was the wrong word, but she

felt she'd reached a balance she could live with. She needed human company as well as chimp company. She needed Ginny and Bren in the same sort of way as she needed Lana. She enjoyed human things – cooked food, surfboarding, travel. She'd be going skiing in a couple of months. It wasn't fair to ask her to give all that up.

Or to have to tell Mum she was going to go away and live in Cayamoro and never see her again.

Eva played the tape through to check. It was all right, firm and final . . . but poor Grog. She turned the tape over and filled the other side with chit-chat about things that had happened while he'd been away and then ill – the fight with Tatters, Mum's most tiresome client winning a lottery, Sniff, Mimi's latest rage, Abel's first real knot, and so on. Bright bedside prattle. It was so difficult to imagine Grog being ill. Almost dying, apparently.

Mimi had chartered an air ambulance and flown out and brought him back to the University Hospital, but he'd been too ill for visitors. Eva had called again, because she was due in for her monthly check at Joan Pradesh's lab, and again she'd been told no, but then the hospital had rung back to say Grog was asking for her but she mustn't stay more than five minutes. It sounded as though he must still be pretty bad. Even so, she wasn't ready for the shock.

All his hair had fallen out. His face was the colour of the underside of a fish, with all the flesh wasted from beneath the skin. His eyes were dull, yellow, exhausted, but at least they moved. If he'd had them shut she would have thought he was dead. She realized at once she couldn't give him the tape.

'Hi,' he whispered. 'Good to see you.'

'Uh?' she grunted.

'Had a bad time. My fault. They thought I was done for, but they've got it licked at last. I've had half a million little wrigglers playing lurkie-lurkie round my bloodstream, but they've all gone now. Taught me a lesson. Can't send chimps to Cayamoro. Not got the immunities, any more than I had.'

He closed his eyes. Eva grunted agreement and relief. He didn't notice the relief.

'Going to have to make our own jungle,' he said. 'Nice, clean jungle. On an island, uh?'

With the closed eyes and the whisper it was as if he was talking in his sleep, muttering his dreams. Eva mumbled sounds of doubt. His eyes opened.

'You're against?' he said.

'Uh.'

'Why? Only thing makes sense.'

'Tell you when you're stronger.'

'No. Now.'

of energy in his

told me you're

Right?'

His voice was more than a whisper now, and there was a tinge of pink in his cheeks. It was as if the argument was actually good for him. Eva took the tape out.

'OK,' she said. 'I'm sorry, Grog. Listen to side one when you're feeling stronger. Side two is just chat.'

'Thanks.'

He closed his eyes and sighed. Eva thought he'd fallen asleep, but then his lips moved.

'Have some grapes. More than I can eat.'

It was, too, a huge mound, purple and green. She took a whole bunch and felt her mouth starting to water. Grog smiled.

'Can't promise you they aren't poisoned,' he said. 'Mother keeps sending them.'

Eva had discovered quite a human-sounding chuckle she could do with her own mouth, but she couldn't control it the way she could her voice-box remarks, so now it came out all false.

Her sense of shock and depression deepened as she knuckled along corridors and rode escalators and lifts to Joan's lab. Check-ups had in any case become rather boring by now. Nothing new was likely to happen, so Joan left them to her assistants. They wired you up and made you run on a moving belt and do other sorts of exercise; then, still wired up, you did memory tests and perception tests and intelligence tests; then they showed you shapings of things which were supposed to stir you up in different ways – human and chimp babies, a motor smash, a snake eating a mouse, a nude male model, a bowl of apples, and so on, while the machines you were wired to recorded your pulse and your palm moisture and your brain rhythms and dozens of other things happening inside you and fed the results into computers to be juggled around. Today, by the time she reached

144

this stage, the shapings seemed to mean nothing at all.

'Are you OK, sweetie?' said Minnie. She was a happy, round-faced girl with a sharp little nose and tiny eyes. She was far brighter than she looked, Eva had found.

'Uh?'

'Only you hardly seem to be registering.'

'Sorry. Thinking about something else.'

Just saying so brought back the image of Grog, bald and beardless on the pillow.

'Whup!' said Minnie. 'Something registered there!'

'I visited a friend on the way. He's been very ill. All his hair's fallen out.'

'Too bad.'

'Chimps mind about hair.'

'So you do too?'

'Uh.'

'OK. Let's see if we can find you something nice

. . . . for an

'An utter . . . . . Minnie?'

'She's not been concentrating. She's a bit upset. She's been visiting a sick friend.'

Joan nodded, not interested. She took over the console from Minnie and whizzed through the earlier results, faster than you'd have thought anyone could have taken them in.

'Absolutely normal,' she said. 'I think we can stop doing this – we are not going to get anything new. Of course I am not a psychologist – I can only judge the physiological data. Do you feel yourself to be a fully integrated creature, Eva?'

'Most of the time. Only I get chimp urges I've got to go along with. I'm more chimp than you expected, aren't I?'

Joan said nothing, but stared at the VDU, not really seeing it. She rose.

'We'll disconnect her now, Minnie,' she said.

'We haven't quite finished.'

'Never mind.'

Joan helped remove the sensors with quick and expert fingers. She might be arrogant but she wasn't proud.

'Now, come with me,' she said, and led the way out into the corridor and along to a windowless room, one wall of which was lined with VDUs. Meg was sitting at one of the consoles. She turned and said, 'Hi, Eva,' but her smile was strained and sad.

'I want you to look at something,' said Joan. 'I'm not going to tell you about it, because I don't want to put ideas into your head. If you find it too distressing, you must tell me.'

She pressed a switch. A zone hummed, and at the other end of the room shapes became solid – a hospital bed ringed by machines, the broken web, the thing like a hairy spider at the centre – a chimp's head on the pillow, split by a huge, straining grin. The

146

gleaming canines showed it was a male. The eyes were wide open, staring at the ceiling.

Eva knuckled across to the zone and circled it. So this was what was left of the boy called Stefan and the chimp called Caesar. It could only be them. She felt her lips beginning to strain in sympathy, copying the grin of horror.

To Dad's surprise and Mum's relief Eva had not wanted to talk much about what would happen when Joan's new patients woke. People expected her to be excited at the idea of having companions like herself, but her own feelings were more mixed. There had even been a strand of jealousy in them, at the knowledge that soon she would be losing her own special uniqueness. Fame was funny. You didn't want to share it. But much more important than that had been the fear, half thought and half felt, that having others like her would upset the balance she had achieved. Because there was no one like her, people had to accept her as human when she was with them, ~~~~~~~~~~~~~~ her as chimp when she

So, on the whole, ing about the moment when she would meet Stefan/Caesar. Perhaps that was why, when the moment came, the shock was not the simple, selfish shock of disappointment. It was pure shock, shock at the thing itself.

The bedclothes beside the body moved. 'Erch,' said a voice. 'Gningg.'

Eva knuckled back to Joan.

'Gone wrong?' she said.

'We began the resuscitation procedure nineteen days ago. We had earlier felt able to take a few short cuts on the basis of what we learnt from you, and it is just possible that we made a mistake there, but if so it hasn't shown up in any of our tests. Personally I am confident that the transfer has taken place, that Stefan's axon network has replicated in the animal's brain, that he is, in lay terms, *there*. But for some reason he is unable to communicate, either with the animal's body or through it with the outside world.'

Eva turned and circled the zone again, staring at the image on the imaged bed. No use.

'Can I go in?' she said.

'If you don't mind going through the sterilizer.'

'You won't have to do my clothes.'

Eva stripped and stood in the little cubicle. Her hair bushed out around her under the tingling bombardment. She opened the inner door and went through. The room was just the same as when she used to lie here, with the bed and the mirror and the silent machines, and beyond the window the huge sky with the city stretching away beneath it. She pulled a stool over to the bed and climbed on to it, so that she could lean over and peer down into the dark eyes. There was nothing she could read there, no presence, no signal. Her hand moved without her telling it to and began to groom through the long black hairs on the scalp.

'He hasn't got any feeling there,' said Meg's voice. 'Just his left arm and his mouth.'

Eva shifted the bedclothes back. The hand lay across a keyboard just like hers. Sometimes the fingers twitched, and when they touched the 'speak' key a voice came out, meaningless. She settled herself and started to groom her way painstakingly up the arm. Was there a faint response, felt through her fingertips, as though the flesh itself recognised the signal? But when she peered into the eyes again she saw no change, and the agonized grin stayed tense.

She lifted the twitching fingers aside and pressed the keys.

'Hi,' said a boy's voice from the keyboard speaker. 'I'm Stefan. I'm here. I'm OK.'

The arm threshed at the sound, straining against the straps that held it.

'That is his regular reaction,' said Joan out of the air. 'Violent agitation.'

Eva let the threshings subside and returned to ~~~ she imagined she

Eva grunted ~~~ him to go back into darkness with the feel of ~~~ fingers on his flesh. It seemed important, she didn't know why. She felt the change in her fingertips and looked up in time to see the eyes close, the lips lose their tension, soften and close too, until the face was

149

that of a young male chimp, asleep, deep in a dream – a dream, perhaps, of trees.

Totally exhausted Eva knuckled out into the control room and put on her overalls. She was very shivery. While she had been in the bedroom she had been too busy, too absorbed in trying to make contact, to understand quite what she had seen and felt. Now the horror of it gathered inside her and exploded into a howling hoot. She rocked herself to and fro in her misery. Joan stood watching, bright-eyed, but Meg jumped off her chair, knelt down and cuddled beside her, sobbing with human grief.

Eva recovered first and reached for her keyboard.

'Sorry,' she said. 'Couldn't help it.'

'We are all somewhat shaken,' said Joan. 'Do you have any ideas?'

'They're both there. They don't want each other.'

'Both?'

'Stefan. Caesar. Like Kelly's here.'

She tapped herself on the chest.

'I made myself want Kelly,' she said. 'I knew I had to. Suppose it's easier for me. Always been used to chimps.'

'I'm afraid that may well be the answer,' said Joan. 'At a very early age, thanks to your father's decision to bring you up in such close contact with the Pool, you may well have learnt to think of yourself as actually being a chimpanzee as well as a human, and that deep in your subconscious mind you still do so. The attraction of this theory is that the level at which rejection of the transfer is most likely to occur is very close to the subconscious, the boundary where the human mind has to mesh with the autonomous systems of the animal host.'

The zone had not been switched off. Eva knuckled over and circled it, staring at the thing on the bed. She had her horror under control now, but if anything it was stronger than before. Before, she had simply felt it, in her shivers, in her howling, but now she thought it too. These humans, they couldn't know. They cared, they were sad, but they couldn't understand. This was what humans did to animals, one way or another. This was what they'd always done. The ghastly little wrigglers that had invaded Grog's bloodstream had more right to be there than Stefan had to be in Caesar, or Eva herself in Kelly.

She grunted and turned to Joan.

'So I'm going to be the only one?' she said.

'What do you mean?'

'Nobody else has been brought up with chimps.'

'That is only one theory. In any case we shall have to see.'

'You're going to do *more*?'

'Sasha is due to wake in eleven days, and I shall

lifts and scuttled along

her way back to Grog's room. He was lying as she'd left him, with his eyes closed. The tape was running.

'. . . then what about all the people down at Cayamoro?' her voice was saying. 'The scientists, for instance. They're . . .'

151

YEAR TWO, MONTH THREE, DAY SEVENTEEN

Living with a purpose.
Waking with it already at work in your mind.
Allies, enemies, schemes, failures.
Secrets.
Even in the minute-by-minute life of the Reserve,
thinking all the time.
One day . . . somehow . . .

By the time Grog's beard was long enough to groom
again he could sit up, write letters, talk for an hour at
a time. At the request of Stefan's parents, Joan
Pradesh had put Stefan back into a coma and let him

There was going to be a p
The University was very jumpy about it, because it
was pretty well certain Joan would put everyone's
backs up and then sponsors would get scared and
funds would be cut. So they'd arranged for Eva to be
there too, clever, famous, popular Eva, the whole

world's favourite cuddly toy – if Eva told people it was all right, then the fuss would die down and the funds would go on rolling in and that was all that mattered in the world . . .

'You don't need to worry,' Grog had said. 'There'll be quite a few people on our side down in the audience – I've been rounding them up. If it doesn't come up some other way Mike will ask you a direct question . . .'

'Uh?'

'You'll know him – a blind white blob. Get a few lines ready on your tape. Be nice about Joan. After that just play it by ear. This is our first big chance, but don't let that scare you. They all love you out there, remember.'

Eva was trying not to think about it because it was a waste of her morning in the Reserve. Though she spent every spare minute she had here now, it still wasn't enough – not just because she was happier here, more herself, either. In fact that wasn't true. Visits to the Reserve were sometimes very unsatisfactory, difficult or boring or frightening, harder to control than human life. And human life was a lot of fun, often exciting and interesting, and easier every day as people got used to her . . .

But that was all beside the point. She needed to be at the Reserve more, for the purpose. Suppose the impossible came true, and Grog found a place where they could go, and together they persuaded Dad and the others to let them, to help them when they got there, and all the other parts of the dream slotted in, what would be the use if the chimps themselves weren't ready? You couldn't tell *them* what was going

154

to happen, teach them how to cope, any of that, so 'ready' just meant trusting Eva, being prepared to follow her lead – an outsider, a female, a juvenile, coming and going at random. Not easy.

Winter had been tough. Some days the chimps hardly went out into the open at all, but stayed in their 'caves' squabbling for places nearest the heated patches of wall and floor. In those close unnatural quarters tempers were bad, and the signals for keeping them in control didn't always work. Tatters and Geronimo had several real fights, with serious bite-wounds. By the end of the winter Tatters was boss, which was a bad thing all round, because Geronimo used to use his authority to keep the fights among the females from getting serious by siding with the one who looked like losing, which was why on the whole the females had supported him, but Tatters wasn't clever enough for that. By the time the spring sun was strong enough to lounge and scratch in, the whole group was in a sour mood.

of the time but also glancing

looking for something out of sight of the rest of them. They should have been aware of the danger. Lulu had never managed to rear a baby of her own because her deafness stopped her hearing the cries and whimpers which should have told her its needs, so she couldn't really be trusted near someone else's. Unfortunately Beth was in a cantankerous mood and the other three were preoccupied with watching for a sudden attack from her. The first they knew of the kidnapping was Wang's chittering scream as Lulu dashed away, dragging him by one arm and bashing him casually against the hard ground as she went.

Lana raced after her, shrieking, with Eva close behind. They galloped round the corner of a slab and stopped dead because Tatters was there, facing them, with his hair bushed out and his face drawn into a hoot. Beth and Beth's group had supported Geronimo longer than any of the other females, and Tatters hadn't yet forgiven them. Lulu settled down behind Tatters and started grooming Wang, holding him upside down by one leg while he struggled and shrilled. Lana shrieked at Lulu until Tatters rushed at her. Eva raced in to try and grab Wang while his back was turned, but Tatters must have seen what she was up to, because just as she faced Lulu's snarl, looking for an opening, she felt a stunning buffet on the side of her head and was spun sideways across the rough concrete. Before she could rise, Tatters landed on her with all his weight, driving her back to the ground. The breath shrieked out of her. As Tatters jumped to come down again she managed to wriggle sideways so that he half missed his footing, giving her a moment to tumble herself right over into one of the pits and out of sight. By the time Tatters realized what had happened she was out on the far side of the pit and swinging up one of the iron trees.

Tatters was still full of aggression. He could easily have followed her up the tree and continued punishing her there; despite her advantage of being uppermost he would have been much too quick and strong for her, but that was against the rules. He swung round looking for another target. Lulu was crouched where she'd been, licking a bite-wound on her arm and moaning between licks. Wang had gone, and so had Lana, but Geronimo had been sitting all this while (about twenty seconds) with his back to the squabble, pretending not to know it was happening, while Sniff had been perched a little further off, as usual watching the whole scene.

Now Tatters knuckled over to Geronimo and began to circle him, hooting, with his hair bushed out. Geronimo, head bowed, watched him out of the corner of his eyes. Geronimo had three options. He could challenge Tatters back, or he could submit by bowing down and panting and letting Tatters step over him, or he could run away up a tree. The tension mounted. Any moment now he would make a dash for it. But then an odd thing happened. Sniff rose,

forward. Tatters stopped dead in looked away. Geronimo hooted again. Tatters hesitated, turned and knuckled away. Geronimo and Sniff settled down to groom each other.

Waiting till Tatters was safely out of sight Eva climbed down the tree, but Sniff must have been watching her, because he instantly left Geronimo and came across to meet her. Eva hadn't seen much of Sniff during the winter. According to the human observers he'd gone off and joined up with a different group in one of the other ruined factories while Tatters and Geronimo were fighting it out, so it didn't seem like him to have behaved as he had just done, especially since he was quite bright enough to know that Tatters would make him pay for it as soon as he could get him alone. Now he looked at Eva gravely. She stayed where she was while he went round and gave her rump a quick sniff, then returned to peer into her eyes again. He grunted quietly to himself, then put out a hand and patted her twice gently, on the side of her cheek. It was not a signal she had ever seen one chimp give another, but she understood at once what it meant. 'Don't worry. I'll look after you.' He grunted again and went back to Geronimo.

Later that morning Tatters came charging into Beth's group, buffeting them aside and rushing away before they could join up to drive him off. Apart from that nothing much happened until it was time for Eva to leave. She found Sniff sitting in the little nook that screened the door. She paused. The obvious thing would have been to greet him briefly and move on, as though she was passing by on her way to somewhere else, but she could see from his whole pose, and the sudden alertness at her arrival, that he had been waiting for her and wouldn't be deceived.

He rose, looked at her, went to the door and rattled the grille, then turned and went to the box that contained the lock. He rapped it with his knuckles, looked at her sharply and held out a hand – 'Show

158

me.' All right, thought Eva, I'm going to need a male I can trust, so I'll have to let him see I trust him. She undid the catch, lifted the lid and punched the code. Sniff watched every detail, but jumped with alarm when the door-lock clicked. Eva opened the door.

Grinning with nerves Sniff peered into the darkness beyond. She switched on the light and led the way through, but he stayed close by the door, excited, frightened, his eyes darting from side to side. Now that she'd made the decision to trust him Eva felt it was important to let him understand as much as he could, so she fetched her overalls from the peg and put them on. Though the policy at the reserve was to keep humans out of sight as much as possible, from time to time they had to intervene in one way or another, so all the chimps would have seen them. They mightn't understand about clothes but they'd know they were something to do with humans.

She turned and faced Sniff. He came a pace closer, put out a finger and touched the butterfly on her

a bar of raisin shortbread in the pocket,
out, unwrapped it, broke it in two and gave him half. He sniffed it and peered at it before he bit, and inspected the wrapping too. It was all typical, though just like any ordinary chimp he insisted on looking in the pocket to see if she had another bar. After that she

sat with him by the door for a grooming-session, and then rose and beckoned him back out into the open. He seemed to understand exactly what was happening. Before she left him she patted his cheek, the way he'd done hers. He grunted and knuckled away without waiting for the door to close behind her.

Joan made a real hash of the press conference, worse than anybody could have guessed. She was aggressive and contemptuous, making it obvious that she despised journalists even more than she despised everyone else, and couldn't accept that they had any business to question the rightness of whatever she'd done. There was a man from the University, tall and handsome with silky white hair, who tried to smooth things out and calm everyone down and put Joan's answers into blander phrases, but he only made things worse. At least you could see Joan was being honest; she stuck her chin out and her eyes flashed and she said exactly what she thought, but the man wriggled and squirmed and tried to slither away from the point and blur everything over. Eva could see Joan becoming increasingly irritated by his efforts to tell people that she didn't really mean what she'd just been saying. Tempers were snapping, when a fat shiny-bald young man with huge thick-lensed spectacles stood up and waited for a pause in the shouting.

'Can we hear from Eva?' he said. 'You have the subject of one of these experiments here. May we hear her views?'

'Well . . .' began the silky man.

'Or is she just here to look pretty?' said Mike.

'That's a very . . .' began the silky man.

Eva was sitting on a stool on the other side of Joan, but she reached out a long arm and grabbed the microphone. The man tried to snatch it back but she was far too strong for him. There was a crackle and rasp from the speakers and she had it. She pressed the 'Speak' button on her keyboard.

'Joan saved some of my life,' said her voice. 'So some of me's glad. But all of me knows she was wrong.'

The silky man had left his chair and come round behind. His hand was reaching for the mike.

'I think, if you don't mind . . .'

Eva turned on him with a snarl. Her teeth snapped shut a millimetre from his wrist. He leapt away as if she'd actually bitten him. Several of the journalists cheered. Mike was still on his feet.

'"Some of me"?' he said.

Eva climbed on to the table. She tapped her chest.

'This belongs to a chimp called Kelly,' she said. 'You people stole it from her. You thought you'd

Joan looked at her and put her hand out, palm up.

'May I?' she murmured.

'You're just another monkey, remember,' said Eva.

It was the gesture, like one of Lana's or Dinks's, that had put the thought into her mind, and she was really only saying it to Joan, but the mike picked the words up loud enough for everyone to hear. There was laughter, and a drop in tension. Joan smiled her thin smile as she took the mike.

'Eva is almost right,' she said. 'I am in fact an ape, not a monkey, and so are chimpanzees. Eva's argument is that one species is not entitled to exploit another, one individual member of a species is not entitled even to save its own life, or the life of its child, at the expense of the life of a member of another species. I'm afraid this is nonsense. I would point out that when there were still wild chimpanzees they hunted and ate any small monkeys they could catch, whereas for humans to eat monkeys was comparatively uncommon. Most civilized people would have regarded eating anything so human-seeming with revulsion, and among primitive peoples it was often taboo, even in areas where monkeys were common and meat a luxury. What I might call our unconscious moral standards in these matters are already quite high. It is unlikely that a chimpanzee would have any such qualms. And when it comes to my own work I of course recognize that I must also exercise conscious moral standards. I certainly have no right to expend the life of a member of another species on frivolities. But I have no doubt at all that I had, and have, the right to do so in order to save a human life, as I did for Eva.'

She saw Eva's fingers move on the keys, and paused.

'Not to save my life. Just to know.'

Joan nodded.

'All right,' she said, 'though that is not entirely fair. I was delighted for Eva and her parents when our first

162

transfer succeeded. Eva herself could tell you how unhappy I was about what had happened in the case of Stefan, and of Sasha . . .'

'Caesar?' interrupted Eva. 'Angel?'

'Who? Oh, the two chimpanzees. No, my feelings about them are different, and I would maintain quite properly so. Their lives have not been wasted. We have learnt less than we hoped from them, but we might have learnt a great deal and that is my justification. In this case the knowledge might have led almost immediately to the saving or prolonging of human life, but when my father began his work with flat-worms such an outcome could not have been foreseen. Flatworms are fairly primitive lifeforms, and no doubt some of you would want to draw a line somewhere on the scale between them and the chimpanzees, above which it would be improper to use the animal. This makes no sense to me. I do not know how many flatworms died in the course of our exper-
~~nts — the~~ figure must have run into thousands –
~~of them~~ died unnecessar-

despairing, her big ~~~~
had looked at her, but they hadn't listened. They weren't interested. All most of them wanted to do was to get the conference back to the humans, to Stefan and Sasha and what had happened to them, and how ghastly it must have been for their families,

163

and so on. 'One at a time, one at a time,' the silky man kept saying.

As the shouting rose Eva bowed her head. She was wearing a pair of yellow overalls, Mum's latest, light-weight because of the shaper-lights, with a huge green-and-purple butterfly on the bib. The shouts and arguments – Mike and Grog's other friends were still trying to ask questions about chimp rights – had their usual effect of making her pelt prickle and bush out, so that she could feel the pressure of the overalls enclosing her. She felt like a bubble, a bubble of frustration and anger, and now the bubble seemed to be inside her, rising up, so that she had to leap to her feet and face the human pack and let the bubble burst out in one loud bark, which echoed round the room in the sudden silence.

It wasn't enough. She had to do or say something more. They were waiting. Not words, nothing human. Deliberately she let her inward urges loose. Her hands gripped the hem of her bib and dragged it up until she could nick the point of a corner tooth into the cloth. She pulled down. The hem gave. Using all her strength she ripped the overalls apart right down to the crotch and let go. The yellow cloth crumpled round her ankles. She stepped out of the mess and knuckled away naked along the table, past Joan, past the silky man where he sat clutching the micro-phone, down off the table and out of the room. Behind her she heard the trance of silence break. She did not glance back. The bay of the human pack dwindled along the corridor.

YEAR TWO, MONTH FIVE, DAY NINE

Living with human grief . . .
The wreck of half their hopes . . .
The loss, almost, of their love . . .
Sharing the wreck, the loss, the grief . . .
But living with other hopes and other loves . . .
Living with a purpose.

You reach a sort of calm where you all accept that what's done's done, but there's no going back to where you were before. When Mum comes home from work you fetch her her vodka and orange and give her a hug, but you don't sit in her lap and finger

The morning after the pl . . .
Callaway had come round. She had telephoned before and asked Mum and Dad to stay at home, and for Eva not to go to school. She explained that by publicly criticizing Honeybear for dressing chimps up in human clothes Eva had broken important clauses

in the contracts with World Fruit and SMI. They would overlook it this time, but they were going to insist on a strict code from now on, about what Eva was allowed to do or say. If she broke any of this code, they wouldn't just cut off funds to the Pool and Eva's company, they would also sue Eva's company for damages. Eva's company had no assets except Eva herself, and she was highly valuable. The legal question of who she belonged to was still unresolved, so any lawsuit was likely to be extremely expensive, and might end with Eva finding that she belonged to SMI, a piece of property they could do what they liked with . . .

Eva was amazed. She'd known before she got home that Mum was going to be upset – very upset – and Dad might be angry, which he had been. But this level of fuss! It was almost mad, except that Mum and Dad didn't seem quite so surprised.

'Now is this all quite clear to you too, Eva?' Miss Callaway had said.

'On a chat show or something – if they ask me?'

'You must support the policies and products of the companies in question.'

'Uh uh.'

'In that case you had better refuse invitations to appear on programmes other than those in which an agreed list of questions are adhered to. This will somewhat restrict your appearances, I'm afraid.'

'OK. Provided they don't stop me going to the Reserve.'

Miss Callaway didn't know about the Reserve and looked blank.

'If you must,' said Mum.

'Out of harm's way,' said Dad.

'I must further emphasise,' said Miss Callaway, 'that SMI own complete rights in all reproductions of any performance by Eva, and this includes the unfortunate episode last night. They will refuse permission for all future showings of it, and any such showings will be illegal. All tapes will be regarded as pirated, and their owners prosecuted. Any support by you for such a showing, public or private, will be treated as a breach of the contract, with the consequences I have spoken of. I expect you recorded the conference – may I have the tape, please?'

It was still in the shaper. Eva hadn't seen it – she'd been waiting for a moment when Mum wasn't around. Now Dad took it out without a word and gave it to Miss Callaway, who put it in her briefcase and left. She hadn't said anything about Grog that time. That came later.

Eva had only begun to understand what she'd done

cussion on animal rights, but Eva had told him she wasn't allowed to.

On the news programmes that evening rival companies had shown pictures of chimps, and extinct animals, and were snide about the fact that SMI was refusing permission to let anyone show the sequence.

Grog had called. It was difficult with Mum in the room, so Eva had answered mainly with grunts.

'How's things?'

'Mmmm.'

'Lil and Dan not too happy?'

'Uh.'

'Tell them I'm sorry – no better not. From my point of view it was . . . hell, Eva, I'd never guessed – I was just keeping my fingers crossed and you came up with *that*!'

'Uh?'

'Not seen it yet?'

'Uh uh.'

'You'd better be quick. SMI are going flat out to suppress every damn tape. Anyway, it's just what I wanted. We're off. I'm setting up office tomorrow.'

'Uh!'

(The idea of Grog in an office was a contradiction in terms.)

'Sure. You've opened the gates. It's a tide. It's a wave. Now we've got to ride it. Seeing you.'

He hung up.

'Grog?' Mum had asked.

'Uh.'

'It's all his fault.'

Three days later a letter had come from Miss Callaway saying that any attempt on Eva's part to see or talk to Giorgio Kennedy or any persons connected with any organization set up by him for the return of chimpanzees to a natural habitat would be treated as a breach of the contract.

So, from then on, no Grog, not face to face. Eva saw him quite a bit on the shaper, though, leading marches, lobbying politicians, addressing meetings. The cameras wouldn't be interested in him, but he always seemed to have one of their darlings along with him, some singer, some sports star, some billionaire's boyfriend. Before long the demos were big enough to attract the shaper cameras in their own right. There were banners with slogans, and a symbol – not a chimp but a broken butterfly, one bright wing ripped apart. More and more you saw the same symbol sprayed on to walls as you were driven around the city. Kids at school started coming for autographs again, bringing cards with the broken butterfly printed in one corner.

'Uh uh,' Eva said, and explained that she wasn't allowed to, but she signed a separate piece of paper for them to stick on to the card later. Grog had been right, she realized. The movement was a wave. She could feel it all the time now, in the way people reacted to her. The singers and sports stars were only the glitter at the crest, but underneath came the growing

'Uh?'
'You come here, to my apartment? Tuesday morning.'
'I thought we were doing an ad.'
'Is cancelled. That stupid Grog.'
'Uh?'

169

'All his fault. You come?'

'You know I'm not allowed to talk to him?'

'Is in Berlin. No time for his poor Mama. That boy!'

'How is he?'

'Is well. Is happy. Is boring – I send a car.'

'OK.'

Mimi's flat was almost a mile in the air. A real butler answered the door.

'Miss Venturi is not yet home,' he said. 'If you do not mind waiting.'

He showed Eva into the living room. It was almost dark, because the blinds were down, shutting out what must have been a stupendous view. Grog was sitting in an armchair reading a file.

Eva hesitated a moment, then scuttled across the carpet and leapt into his lap. He laughed and ran his fingers across her pelt. Eagerly she began an inspection of his new beard.

'Great to see you,' he said. 'You don't have to worry – Mother smuggled me in.'

'Sh. Cormac's in the hall.'

'I've told Bill to settle him down in front of a good loud space-epic. How's things? Difficult at home?'

'Uh.'

'Poor Lil – wish. I could talk to her.'

'No good.'

'Not yet – some day, maybe. I've been in touch with Dan – he'll swing round.'

'Huh!'

'We're going to need him. He knows a lot of essential stuff. When he finds where the future's going, he'll join. I don't mean just to stay working. He's enough of a scientist to want to be where the real stuff is happening. Now sit still. There's something I want to show you. I'm just back from a demo in Berlin – our biggest yet. I've got a tape. Look.'

He switched the shaper on. The zone filled with people walking towards the camera, ten abreast. It closed in on a tiny figure in the front rank, blue eyed, golden-haired, wearing a pair of green overalls with a broken butterfly on the bib. Eva recognized her at once – Tanya Olaf had rocketed up the charts out of nowhere five months ago and stayed at the top ever since.

'Whoo!' said Eva.

'Looks good in our rig,' said Grog.

Eva caught a glimpse of him marching in the rank behind, a little to the left. She felt a silly pang of jealousy – since she'd been stopped going on chat-shows she hadn't been meeting people like Tanya.

'What's she like?' she said.

Eva had snorted because the

The camera had swung up and at the same time withdrawn until Tanya and Grog and the other leaders had dwindled to inch-high figures at the bottom of the zone and behind them she now could see, stretching away down the tree-lined boulevard, out of sight in the distance but still coming on, thousands beyond thousands, the rest of the march.

'Good moment,' said Grog.

'You got all those people out?'

'*You* got them out. Didn't you realize? I've just been working on the results.'

The scene jumped. It was dusk now, a different street, the march going by, singing, faces under the lamp-glare, the broken butterfly everywhere. And now it was a sports arena, every seat full and a solid mass of people crammed on to the central space around a floodlit stage. The music stopped and the lights went out. Silence, and then a bay of cheering as a public zone sprang up on the stage – a table draped with blue cloth, a woman speaking into a microphone, on one side of her a grey-haired man with a fretful look and on the other, sitting up on the table in a withdrawn huddle, a chimp in yellow overalls.

There was a curious note in the cheering, not just excitement but challenge.

'First time we've risked it in public,' said Grog.

'I've never seen it.'

'You haven't! *They* all have.'

The woman sat down. The man grabbed the microphone. The heads of journalists bobbed in the foreground. In the sudden silence you could hear their calls, and the man bleating, 'One at a time, please.' You could feel the huge crowd holding its breath, waiting. The chimp jumped to her feet and barked. The sound was like an explosion, ringing out and then echoing off the cliffs of the arena. The cameras closed in till she filled the zone, staring at the crowd. Her rage, her misery, were solid things, as tangible and visible as the table beneath her. She paused, and then with a single firm movement gripped the bib of her overalls in both hands, lifted the hem to her mouth, bit, and tore. The rasp of the rending cloth filled the night. The bright butterfly fell in two. With her black pelt shining under the lights as if electric with animal energies the chimp knuckled along the table, blotting out the two humans as she passed them, and was gone.

The cheering rose, the roar of the human wave. There was a new note in it now, more than the challenge to the fat-cat companies which had been trying to suppress the tape, a sense of excitement, of something special and extraordinary having happened. Eva could feel it too, with her human mind. A message had been passed, an immense gap bridged. The movements of the chimp on the table had expressed what Eva had felt at the conference – she'd known that at the time – but she now saw that they said much more. They spoke for Kelly, and the other

'Therefore not great moment...

'Just don't talk crap, Mother,' said Grog.

She sprang forward, her red cape swirling behind her, a handful of bangles swinging like a knuckle-duster. Eva jumped clear in time for Grog to catch the flailing arm by the wrist and pull his mother down into his lap, where he pinioned her close. It was clearly a movement they'd had plenty of practice at.

'You say crap to your mother – you who are snatching the bread from my mouth!'

'Hey! So it's right about the bread!'

'Already I told you! The banana-merchants are trying to cancel my contract! They will pay me in blood! Eva, call McAulliffe!'

'Uh?' said Eva.

'Her lawyer,' said Grog. 'She calls him nine times a day. Now wait a moment, Mother. I'm going to let you go, and if you bite me Eva's going to bite you right back. Show her your teeth, Eva – give them a good gnash. Ouch! You . . .! Get her, Eva!'

Mimi was on her feet, calmly undoing the clasp of her cloak. With a queenly gesture she flung it over Grog and turned smiling to Eva. Eva snickered back at her. She liked Mimi – Mimi would have got on well in the Reserve, she thought. Grog tossed the cloak aside and sat licking his forearm.

'Let's get this straight,' he said. 'Honeybear are definitely trying to stop the chimp-ads because our boycott is beginning to pressure them?'

'I will not pressure them only, I will massacre them! Get me McAulliffe!'

'Hold it, hold it. What are they going to do instead? Why can't they go back to the series they had you lined up for before Eva came along?'

'Because the little poof who dreamed it up has gone off to new agency, using same idea for different yucky drink.'

'So they're stuck. Great. It's a bit early but we've got to ride the wave. We've got to have some kind of success to show our people, or the movement's going to fold. Nobody's got any staying-power any longer. OK. Mother, you really reckon you can make yourself enough of a nuisance to World Fruit for them to think it's worth buying you off?'

'You never read your old mother's contracts? Works of art! Works of art!'

'Right, you can carry on massacring them till they buy you off by giving you some kind of control over the next series of chimp-ads.'

'Uh!' said Eva.

'Don't worry,' said Grog. 'I've got it all worked out, I hope. We've got to be lucky, but if we all push in the right direction we might swing it. I'm going to offer World Fruit a deal. I can't call off the boycott – too much of a let-down – but I can tell them we'll play it down provided they announce that when they've finished this series of ads they will shoot a new series in a natural location using chimps behaving the way chimps used to in the wild.'

. . . . said Mimi. 'Me, a

work into your contract . . . .
ally settle for is a place called St Hilaire.'

'Uh?' said Eva.

'Island off Madagascar. Extinct volcano. Used to be solid forest, till it was felled a couple of hundred years ago. Now it's bare rocks, apart from a few pockets of real old trees the loggers couldn't reach. It's no good for tourists, no beaches and hot as hell, with the odd cyclone thrown in in a bad year. And it belongs to World Fruit. There's one bit of flat land where they've got a cocoa plantation, but it's never been economically viable and now they've got a virus. The point is it's just about the only location they *can* use. There's patches of trees which are small enough to enclose. My movement can insist on a genuinely natural location, and the chimps having time to get used to being there. Even World Fruit aren't going to get permission to move into somewhere like Cayamoro. What d'you think, Eva?'

Eva shrugged. It seemed so trivial, this stuff about ads and sponsors, after what she'd just seen on the shaper. Was this all that that marvellous surge of human energy, that great wave of love and hope and anger, was going to produce? What difference would it make when the filming was over? A few eased human consciences. Nothing that mattered. Eva didn't understand Grog's excitement at all. Anyway there were all sorts of problems he didn't seem to have thought of. She started with an obvious one.

'Chimps behaving as chimps. They don't know how.'

'Who don't?'

'Jenny and the others. Trained to wear clothes. Only know what it's like in the Public Sector.'

'So we can't take *them* – that's why we'll be taking chimps from the Reserve. Lana, Dinks, Sniff . . .'

'Whuh!'

'You'll have to pick the others. Two males beside

176

Sniff, and that'll mean a dozen females, won't it? Youngsters and babies.'

'Whuh?'

'You're not going to St Hilaire just to shoot a few ads. You don't imagine that's all I've been sweating my guts for, or why I got you along here now? Listen . . .'

Eva listened. Her pelt stirred. Her human mind kept telling her it could never work, never even begin, but while Grog talked her body became restless with excitement and she prowled the rich room, imagining shadows, imagining odours, imagining trees.

YEAR TWO, MONTH TWELVE, DAYS TWO AND THREE

Living in a new world . . .
Heavy, vegetable odours . . .
Racket of insects, clatter of birds . . .
Heat . . .

Dopey still with drugs the chimps stared at the daylight. They felt the steamy heat, breathed the strange air. Their yesterday – nearly three days ago, in fact – had been spent huddled into the caves of the Reserve, with wind-whipped snow scurrying around the concrete outside. They had slept through the flights and stopovers. Only Eva – awake for the journey – had seen the various changes until the final airboat had slanted out of tropic blaze into a ridged mass of cloud, felt its way down through the murk and emerged over a huge dark sea. She had not seen the island until they circled to land, but then there it was. She had pressed her muzzle to the window, misting the glass with her breath. At first what she saw hadn't made sense, but then she had realized that what she was looking at was mainly a mountain rising almost directly from the sea, with its top all fuzzed out by the cloud-base. Below that, desolation, vast jumbled slopes of bare brownish storm-eroded rock. Only here and there darker streaks and patches, the fragmentary remains of what had once been forest before the trees had been stripped away for timber or firewood, or simply for a patch of fresh earth somebody hoped to raise a couple of crops from before the summer rains washed it away; but in these few places, in ravines and on slopes too steep to reach, the last trees still stood.

The flight-path curved on. A flatter, greener area appeared. The sea came nearer, slow ocean rollers freckled with foam. Surf along rocky shores, buildings round a small harbour, trees in patterned rows, touchdown . . .

That had been Eva's yesterday. She could have slept in a bed, but chose to spend the night with the still-doped chimps so that she should wake among them, be already one of them as they first moved out into this other world. She had woken before any of the others, and seen Colin bending over Lana, taking her pulse, lifting an eyelid.

'Uh?'

. . . 'll be glad to

They'll all be whooping about

I'm looking forward to this – it's really something.'

Eva had grunted agreement. The same excitement ran through the whole team. They all felt themselves to be doing something extraordinary, even though it was only three weeks (they thought) and then back to

179

the city, to winter, and the chimps huddling again in the caves of the grim Reserve. But for the moment it was as though they felt they were in at the birth of a new world, with the old tired world waiting and watching. Even the cameramen, who had seen so much they never admitted they were impressed by anything, couldn't quite hide their excitement.

But in Eva's case there was more than excitement, there was fear too, dry mouth, crawling pelt, drumming heart, cold weight in the stomach. She wasn't planning to make her move for at least ten days, but the thought and the fear were there. She watched Wang finger sleepily at Lana's side. Dinks's two-month-old, Tod, was stirring too – the vets had had to give the babies smaller and more frequent shots, so they woke more readily. Colin left. Eva followed him out and was watching him lower the door of the next crate when she heard a quiet snort close behind her. She spun round and saw Sniff's face peering through the door of the crate Colin had already visited. She knuckled over, crouched and greeted him. There was no Tatters here, no Geronimo. Sniff would have to sort out with Billy and Herman who was boss. They were older and stronger. It was important to build up his confidence.

He acknowledged her greeting with a grunt but continued to stare out at the scene beyond. She settled beside him in the doorway, looking at it too, seeing it now as far as she could with his eyes, this totally strange place, nothing like anything he'd known.

What did he see? A patch of reddish jumbled scree sloping down towards him – nothing square, nothing flat, nothing he was used to. Beyond that, dusty green hummocks – bushes – on one side. Denser green – thick growth round a scurry of water. Red scree sloping sharply up on the left. Beyond all that much taller green, dark shadow – trees. Buzz of insects, reek of tropic growth, steamy air under low sky. A bird, bright yellow, dipping across, calling wheep-wheep-wheep. Sniff was shivering with excitement and alarm. Eva groomed for several minutes along the twitching surface of his upper arm, then rose, knuckled a few paces forward, turned and held out her hand, palm up. Come.

He stared, snorted more loudly, took the first pace and halted, his eyes flickering from side to side.

Come.

This time he grunted and followed her up beside the stream, into the shadows. Behind them the hidden cameras watched them go. It was about twenty minutes before they returned to wait for the others to ⬚⬚ ⬚⬚⬚ them out and show them what they had

⬚⬚⬚ trapped the pockets ⬚ could begin. The lower end of this patch ⬚⬚⬚ sided valley, thick with shrubs and saplings. Further up it closed to a sheer-walled ravine, beyond human reach, where older trees still rooted deep into the rock. Out of sight over the bare ridges either side ran a tall electric fence. The humans camped in the dying plantations almost a mile below.

There were remote controlled cameras hidden throughout the area. The idea was that everything the chimps did would be filmed, with Eva helping by seeing they were often in camera-range and also by setting up events and interactions to stimulate them. SMI would edit the film for wildlife programmes and suitable sections would also be dubbed with sophisticated human voices and used for ads for Honeybear. There ought to be enough in the can after three weeks' filming for everyone to go home. It was silly, trivial, a total waste of time and money, but none of that mattered.

It had looked as if it was going to matter at first. When they'd found what it was going to cost, the accountants had tried to put their foot down, but by then the news had got out (Grog's friends had seen to that) that World Fruit were planning to take twenty chimps to a natural habitat for an experimental period, and see what happened. The bare rumour had done more for their sales than a whole season of commercials. From being world-villains they found themselves world-heroes. The expedition was news. By nightfall billions of eyes would have seen that first shot, the dark shapes of two chimpanzees knuckling in silence away into the trees.

Lana was awake, inspecting Wang. Abel was already at the door, peering out bright-eyed, too young to be frightened. Dinks was stirring. The stale reek of the crate was horrible after the live air. Eva beckoned from the door to Lana, who huddled back against the

There had been a lot of discussion back home about whether and how to feed the chimps during the experiment. Botanists on the preliminary expedition to the island had reported that there was enough food in the ringed patch to support twenty chimps for three weeks, provided they knew what to look for. Probably only some of the leaves were edible, and one particular bush was fairly poisonous but tasted so bitter that you knew at once and spat it out. (Eva had tested some of the samples the botanists had brought home.) There were wild fig-trees, and mangos which must have seeded from crop-trees planted by people before the mountains went bald. There were roots too, probably, if you knew what to look for, and ants' nests, and grubs under the bark of old trees up the ravine. Three hectares wasn't a lot for twenty chimps – it would be looking fairly bashed-around by the time they left. Eva had been specially interested in everything the botanists could tell her. It was going to be more important than people knew. But for the moment she was thankful that Dad and the others had decided they would have to come in at night while the chimps were sleeping and leave extra food around.

She knuckled over to Herman and put her muzzle close to the fist that clasped the leaves. He cuffed her casually away – he was a big young male, strong and not very intelligent, but placid and with less than the usual share of male chimp mischief. Sniff had seen the exchange. He snapped a few twigs from the bush and passed them to Eva, who took them and munched experimentally. The taste was faintly nutty, and all but the young leaves at the tips took a lot of chewing.

Not many vitamins there, she guessed. Not much else, either. Chimps in the wild, Dad said, used to spend two-thirds of their day looking for food and the rest eating it when they'd found it.

By now the rest of the group had gathered round and were snatching twigs from the tree and trying the bushes nearby. Billy found a bitter one and spat the leaves out with a grunt of disgust, then went and washed his mouth out in the stream. They were used to being fed in their caves soon after they woke, so they kept making trips back to the crates to see whether breakfast had come yet. Eva was hungry too, but waited. She felt it was important that she shouldn't always be the one who did things first.

In the end it was Sniff. He took Herman by the wrist and led him to the gap in the bushes he and Eva had found earlier. At the opening he turned and beckoned to Eva. Come. She rose and signalled to Lana and Dinks, but it was Abel, who nowadays associated Eva in his mind with amusements and games, who
followed, tut-tutting,

berries, and some
dead leaves – they tasted like shrimps without
flavour – and a bog-plant with long pale leaves whose mid-rib you could crunch like celery. They had also begun to learn that trees were not as easy to climb as they looked, especially if you were used to the rigid

185

steel branches welded to the pillars of the reserve. Herman had one crashing fall into the bushes below and rose bewildered, still clutching the branch that had snapped on him. By that time they'd eaten enough for the moment, and it was getting too hot to move, so they rested.

There were two trees of the same kind, with smooth grey many-forked branches, growing low down from opposite cliffs of the ravine and meeting over the rush of water. Two hidden cameras up in the cliffs were trained on the place, but Eva hadn't needed to coax the others there. They had found it of their own accord and swung themselves up, draping their bodies into crooks and crotches, making a pattern of dark strong shapes against the snaking grey branches. They twitched, or scratched, or groomed for a while at a neighbour, or moved lethargically to a fresh perch or to join another chimp, but for the most part they stayed still.

Eva sat at the edge of the group and watched them. Deliberately she lived in the moment, refusing to think about what lay ahead. She could not imagine that she would ever be so happy again, so filled with tingling, sparkling peace. Of course it was too hot for scampering round, though the spray from the stream helped, but she could feel that there was more to the stillness of the chimps than that. It was something shared, like a song, the wonder, the amazement, the deep content, the sense of having come home. She did not have to guess but knew, because she could feel the awareness going to and fro between them, shared and real, that they understood what had happened. The part that mattered, anyway. All of them, wide awake,

186

were remembering and recognizing the dream. If nothing else happened, or everything she and Grog had planned went wrong, this hour, this noon, would have been worthwhile.

In the early afternoon Eva experimented with making herself a nest. She was going to have to teach the others, so it was important to get it right herself first. It was easy, once you'd learnt to recognize the sort of branches needed, close and whippy enough to bend and then lace together, holding them in place with your weight. Later still she seemingly accidentally coaxed the chimps up the southern slope outside the ravine to where the humans had left the day's rations – mostly plain chimp-chow, with enough bananas to go round. Sniff and Billy had their first set-to, not a proper fight, but bluffing and challenging, and then, before anything serious happened, settling down to intense close mutual grooming. They were still at it when the rain started.

It came almost in an instant, a few large drops rat-

...crashing down-

as a flivver lifted them away

stared at the blank space in dismay. The stream was roaring now with a dangerous sound, which added to their alarm. Across the valley, below where the crates had been, stretched the electric fence.

The fence had become the biggest problem in the

whole expedition. The sponsors nearly called it off because of the cost and difficulty, but everyone had agreed that without one the chimps would probably go roving across the barren mountain to other patches of forest, almost impossible for humans to reach, and be lost completely. Even as it was, the whole programme was months late, because the fence had taken so long to build. There should have been sun, and sparkling waters, instead of this day-long mug.

Now the chimps gazed at the fence and the barren slope beyond. To their minds there was no other place the crates could have gone but down there. Several of them knuckled over to the fence to look, naturally enough reaching hands to grip the mesh as they did so. They leapt back with barks of dismay, then gingerly reached forward and tried again, snatching their hands back at the first tingle. Some of them perhaps knew about electric fences, because there were places round the Reserve where possible escape routes had been blocked with charged wire, but they wouldn't all have explored that far.

The rain, if anything, was heavier now. For a few minutes they scuttered to and fro along the fence, as if hoping for a gap. Sniff, more purposefully, traced the line up the right-hand ridge and over to where it turned and climbed towards the cloud-base. He paused in the angle, staring out over the barren, horrible rockscape, all streaming with thousands of individual tiny waterfalls, then snorted and turned away. Eva had followed, interested both in the fence and in Sniff's reactions, and when he saw her he snorted on a slightly different, negative, note, and led the way back down into the valley. The others were already heading up into the comparative shelter of the trees.

In the ravine the stream was a foaming fawn torrent, but near its lower end rose a stand of broad-leaved palms, with dryish patches beneath them. Here they huddled together, their drenched pelts steaming. Night fell, and suddenly they were in total dark. By the time the rain stopped, an hour later, they were all asleep, but Eva, restless, woke and saw lights moving around. Her first thought was that Dad or some of his helpers had come up to check that they were all right, but then she realized that the lights were too faint and there were far too many of them, hundreds, thousands, blinking their different codes. Fireflies. Of course. She lay for a little, listening to the roar of the stream, and at last fell properly asleep.

Sniff explored the fence in the morning. Eva had expected him to, just as he seemed to have expected her to come round with him. It was another steamy

at the mountainside, all brownish dull rock and glaring with the heavy diffused light, plunging towards the sea. From up here you could see the plantation spreading across the three square miles of plain at the foot of the mountain, the regular green rows mottled brown with the disease.

During one of his pauses Sniff gazed at the area with deep interest, then grunted, nudged Eva and pointed, not at the plantation, but out beyond to the tip of the island, the little harbour with a ship loading, and in an open patch beside the buildings the SMI airboat tethered firm and the two flivvers, tiny as toys with distance. His snort expressed wariness and distrust.

The fence turned again, running sideways across the slope now, and climbed steeply to cross the ridge which lower down became the left-hand flank of their valley. At the crest Sniff halted. This was the highest point of the enclosure. From here you could see a whole new expanse of mountain, almost the same as the other side, but steeper, with sheer cliff in places and in others loose rock at such a slope that it seemed poised for a fresh fall. There was another difference. About a mile away, nearer to the peak, was a large patch of dull green – trees.

They were too far off for Eva to tell whether they were real trees, or just bushes which had somehow retained their root-hold on the incredible slope, but she could understand why they'd never been cleared – there was almost no way any human could reach them. She stared and stared. It was no use trying to work out a possible route – too much of the slope between was hidden – but she couldn't help trying. 'Take as many of the others as you can with you,' Grog had said. 'If the worst comes to the worst you'd have to go alone. Give me a month.' Grog had never been on the island – he'd only seen photographs. From them it looked as if there'd be places to hide, and enough to eat. He couldn't have known.

She heard Sniff grunt, and turned. He was already climbing back down the ridge towards the ravine. Eva waited. She heard him crashing about below, and then he came back carrying a small branch he had torn from a bush. When he reached the fence he put the branch against it, at first just brushing the leaf-tips quickly along and then withdrawing it. Feeling no shock he pushed harder. The mesh bowed out under his weight, but the fence had been engineered to stand such attacks – Dad would know that the chimps were quite clever enough to try something like that if they chose – and the branch broke first.

Sniff wasn't ready. He fell solidly against the wire and got the full force of the current. All his hair shot erect. He jumped back and might have gone tumbling helplessly down towards the stream if Eva hadn't

it minutely, his muzzle only a few inches away from the mesh. After a while, with a grunt of disappointment he continued their exploration down the slope, but now didn't pause either to test the current or to look at the mountain.

Just as they were gathering for their midday rest in the ravine a whooping noise began from down the slope. It was in fact the recorded call of a howler monkey, chosen because it was natural enough not to alarm the chimps but couldn't be mistaken for anything else. If it had come in short bursts it would have been a signal that Dad or someone wanted to see her, urgently, but the steady unbroken version just meant 'Come if you can.' Sniff had come back from his reconnoitre in an aggressive mood and had had several confrontations with Billy. Now they were making it up, clasped together, absorbedly peering and combing each other's fur. Nobody but Sniff would have been likely to keep an eye on Eva. Slowly she edged herself clear and slipped away.

Dad was waiting by the gate, fanning the flies away with a branch. Sweat streamed down his beard.

'Having fun?' he said.

Eva grunted enthusiasm.

'And your pals?'

'Uh.'

'The shaper chaps are pleased with the pictures they're getting. There's one long sequence, yesterday, when you were settling into those trees in the gorge. That was lovely to see. Like a Japanese print.'

He had brought the keyboard. Eva picked it up and pressed the keys.

'Lovely to do,' she said.

Eva had heard the enthusiasm in his voice, and was glad, but at the same time bothered. In a few days' time she was going to let him down, very badly. He was doing his best for her, and for the chimps, he thought. He really wanted them to be happy. He loved them, in his way. Probably he understood them better than any human alive, but still she didn't dare tell him.

'What happened up at the top of the enclosure this morning?' he said.

'Uh?'

'We saw you and Sniff going off on your fence-survey. Characteristic – he's a very bright lad. We've not got any cameras right up there in the open, so next we knew was the alarm bell ringing in the camp. The circuit didn't break, so we left it until we saw you coming back down the far side.'

Inwardly Eva frowned. They hadn't told her about the alarm bell.

'He fell against the fence,' she said. 'He'd been testing it with a branch. He's learnt now.'

'You don't think we ought to get cameras up there?'

'He was just looking. He's like that. They won't run off. They're happy here.'

'That's my line, I must say. I'll be sorry for them

swung across through the branches and faced her, bristling. When she crouched and panted he came close and smelt her all over, then faced her again, less challengingly but with a look of querying suspicion. She reached up and stroked his cheek before offering him her shoulder to groom. He grunted softly and began, while Eva sat hunched and thinking.

The alarm bell was a problem. On the other hand it was good to know for sure that there were no cameras up at the top. She'd been told about the cameras in the valley, because of being expected to manoeuvre the chimps in front of them, so she ought to be able to construct a mental map of the areas which weren't in shot. In one of those areas she'd have to find and break off a long straight branch, preferably with a fork at the end, and strong enough to bear Sniff's weight. Then, still keeping out of shot, she'd have to take it up and stow it somewhere near the top.

Food? It might be possible to hoard some chimp-chow. They'd found enough food in the trees yesterday not to eat all their ration last night. There were no cameras trained on the feeding area, because the whole idea was to show the chimps living wild. Chimp-chow would be a let-down. But how to store it and carry enough to see four or five chimps through the first day or so . . .

Four or five? Well, Sniff would come. Eva was as sure of that as if he'd told her in words. Lana was no adventurer, but she'd have to be made to, somehow. Two more at the most. Who? How?

And when? The obvious time for a break-out was early dawn. With a bit of luck it would be hours before the watchers below were sure enough in their counting to know you were missing, but you'd never get chimps to behave like that. Chimps liked to wake slowly, and sit around and scratch and groom each other, reminding themselves who and where they were, and how they fitted into the group. They'd never be restless enough for action till at least mid-morning, and by then the humans below would be watching . . .

And now the alarm bell . . .

Eva heard a gloomy, meditative grunt and realized

194

that she had made it herself. Sniff stopped grooming. He put his hand to her face and turned her head so that he could stare into her eyes. His gaze was clear, deep and steady. After a while he grunted, using almost exactly the same tone that she had. What was he thinking? Could he actually read her thoughts? There was something shared, anyway, she was certain, not the detailed plans, but at least the idea of escape, and the feelings that went with it. Difficult. Frightening. Necessary.

YEAR TWO, MONTH TWELVE, DAY TEN

Living in tension, waiting . . .
Waking – will the chance come today?
Noon, heat, peace in the ravine, the humans below all
  resting – now?
Not yet.
Dusk, with drenching rain, tree-smell and sea-smell.
Tomorrow . . .?
Perhaps.

Eva heard the howler while she was still trying to settle herself into her pelt for the day, fingering around, nosing and nibbling under the hairs, the way you did. She was conscious of having slept badly, for once, and now her fur didn't seem to want to lie down. The others were uneasy too. She could sense a restlessness, a nerviness. They kept glancing up between the leaves, where the clouds moved low and dark, and faster than usual. Then she heard the signal, a burst, cut short, and another burst, and a gap, and again . . . urgent.

Lana was giving Wang his morning once-over. Sniff was grooming Herman – he'd had a set-to with Billy yesterday which had ended with Billy chasing him up a tree, so now he'd evidently decided to make a serious alliance with the much less ambitious third male.

The others were fidgety, preoccupied. It was no problem to slip away.

She found Dad inside the fence, with the Expedition Coordinator, Maria, and Diego, who'd headed the advance party and built the enclosure. They were all three looking at the sky. Out here you could really see how low and dark the clouds were, and how fast they were travelling. The wind was up too – she hadn't heard it in the ravine because of the noise of the stream. It was like no wind Eva had ever felt, a huge block of steamy heat mov-

Apparently we've got

to evacuate. Maria wants to get the chimps in.'

'I'm getting the crates lifted up,' said Maria. 'If you can get the chimps down here, we'll put some doped fruit out.'

'Uh uh,' said Eva, and took the keyboard from Dad.

'Don't think I can,' she explained. 'I'm not boss. Sniff's having trouble with Billy.'

'Good grief,' said Maria. 'Couldn't we lay a trail of fruit?'

'I doubt if you'd get them all,' said Dad.

'What are you going to do with them?' said Eva. 'When you've got them?'

'Keep them in the crates till it's over,' said Dad in a

flat tone. Knowing him so well, Eva could tell that this was all part of an argument, which he'd lost.

'Uh uh.'

'It's the best we can do,' said Maria.

'Spoil everything,' said Eva.

'It's not just that,' said Dad. 'Just think what it would be like in the crates, with a typhoon going on. It wouldn't necessarily be any safer, in my opinion.'

'I told 'em, I told 'em,' said Diego.

'It was getting that damn fence built,' said Maria. 'Listen, Eva, you realize there's every chance that ravine will fill with water, and you'll all be drowned.'

'Uh?' said Eva, looking at Dad. He shrugged.

'Can't tell,' said Diego. 'Must've been cyclones before. The trees in there have stood it.'

'We can climb out, up,' said Eva. 'Blossom found a way.'

'Yes, we saw that,' said Dad.

'Why does something like this *always* have to happen?' said Maria. 'Every damn project I've ever been on. The better it's going, the worse it comes.'

'You might get some terrific pictures,' said Eva.

She said it on purpose. At first she'd just been reacting to the immediate problem, the cyclone, and whether she could get the others down, and what was the best thing to do. But from what Dad had said about the crates not being any safer she'd realized that the human argument wasn't really over, and the more weight she could put on his side the more chance there was of staying. He was right, anyway. Now she'd had time to think she was determined not to do what Maria said. If the worst came to the worst she'd simply disobey orders. It wasn't that she'd

198

planned the escape completely yet, or was sure it would work or that she'd get anyone except Sniff to go with her, but a break like this . . . they'd have to keep the chimps drugged while the typhoon lasted, or they'd go mad in the crates. They might even decide they'd got enough film already and could all go home . . .

Maria was talking into a commo. Diego was watching the sky. All three humans were streaming with sweat.

'Well done,' muttered Dad.

'Too late,' she said. 'They . . . lashed down before then.'

'Tell them to send up more chimp-chow,' said Dad. 'Several days' rations. In a steel box, with a lock. I'll leave the key under that rock, darling.'

'What about the fence?' said Maria.

'Still have to switch the alarm off,' said Diego. 'That amount of wind, it'll keep setting itself off. There'll still be the current, unless we get a lightning strike. They'll lay low, won't they? None of 'em have been near the fence for days.'

'What d'you think, darling?' said Dad.

'Uh?'

It took Eva a moment to gather her wits. The whole problem of crossing the fence without setting off the alarm had filled her waking mind for days. Even when she was dreaming the dream she kept finding her path between the branches blocked by live mesh.

'They wouldn't anyway,' she said. 'Happy where they are.'

'God, if I'd been given a whole day's warning,' said Maria.

'It'll be all right, my dear,' said Dad. 'Personally I think the chimps will be safer up here than we will down on the shore-line. The ravine is good shelter, provided the water doesn't rise too far, and as Eva says, if the worst comes to the worst they can always climb out.'

'Least they won't have tidal waves to look out for,' said Diego.

'I suppose there's that,' said Maria. 'OK. You win.'

'We'll be OK,' said Eva.

'Let's hope,' said Maria. 'You'll be on your own.'

The wind rose unsteadily. At full force you could hear its shriek even above the rush of the stream. In the lower part of the valley the bushes threshed like waves. And then there would be a lull, though the clouds still raced over, lower than ever now. In these pauses Eva's pelt seemed to crawl with electricity. The others, presumably, felt the same. They were all very uneasy, making short expeditions to the nearer feeding-trees and heading back for the ravine after a few mouthfuls. Sniff and Billy seemed to have forgotten their conflict for the moment. Sniff in particular was anxious, and now kept his eyes on Eva most of the time, and followed her around. In one of the lulls she took the chance to lead him, by a route she had worked out to avoid the cameras, up the left flank of the valley to where she had been trying during the last few days to weaken the branch she wanted by gnawing a ring round its base. He studied the bite-marks, frowning, and smelt them too, then looked in a puzzled way along the length of the branch. Eva made the 'Come' signal and led the way on, threading through the scrub-covered slope above where it dropped to the ravine and up on to the bare ridge at the top of the valley, close to the place where Sniff

Eva pointed to the place, and ... g considered the problem, frowning. She could sense him trying to estimate distances. He grunted, doubtfully, then raised his head and stared at the far trees. The upper end of the wooded patch was hidden in the cloud-base. He was still looking when the lull ended. The hot wind came booming off the ocean, so strong now that they had to crouch beneath its weight. When Sniff faced it, it sleeked his pelt like silk, but when he turned for the shelter of the valley the wind got under the fur and bushed it out as if he'd been displaying. He led the way now, following the route they'd taken, down to the tree with the weakened branch. The wind was roaring through the tree-tops, making them bow all one way, like weed in a stream.

Sniff looked at the branch for a few seconds and began to climb. He clambered slantwise up it and gripped another, stouter branch which crossed it about five metres up. With his feet on the lower branch he heaved them apart until he was standing like a triumphant weight-lifter with his arms raised above his head. The branch creaked. Eva gnawed at the straining fibres, feeling them snap as the cut opened. The branch gave with a crash, leaving Sniff dangling in mid-air, but he swung himself up and climbed down, panting not with the effort but with excitement. Together they twisted the branch free and broke off the twigs and side-shoots. Eva wondered whether the microphones had picked up the noise. She guessed so, but the wind would cover most of it, and in any case the chimps did a fair amount of crashing around in the ordinary course of things.

They dragged the branch up the slope and out into the open. The wind was really howling now. A human could hardly have stood in it. When they tried to raise the branch towards the top of the fence it lashed around, unmanageable. Eva would have given up at once – it was too soon, in any case, to get that far, because Diego mightn't have switched the alarm off yet and suppose they did get it in place then Sniff would insist on trying to cross and perhaps get stuck outside. But he'd got the bit between his teeth now, and even with Eva only pretending to help he almost managed it before a sudden new blast of wind made him give up. Crouching under its force he glared at the fence-top and the mountain beyond, then snorted and led the way back.

The others were all in the ravine, huddled together,

nervous, waiting. Down here you could hardly feel the wind, but you could hear its shriek and see the black ominous clouds racing above the threshing tree-tops. The chimps' alarm was like an odour, something they all breathed and shared. Wang clung close to Lana, as if he'd been a baby, and Tod huddled in Dinks's arms with a wide, terrified grin. The same white fear-signal gleamed on every dark face. Eva was grooming Lana, trying to calm her, when the rain

like a flail. You heard the

the branch besid

her own immediate survival. Below

stream leap in its bed. One moment it had been tumbling down its rocky channel in the floor of the ravine and the next it was crashing, white, from cliff to cliff. As the first wall of rain passed by somebody scrambled snorting up beside her – Sweetiepie, drenched and grinning with terror. The opposite tree had one comfortable branch that hung low, only a metre or so above the floor of the ravine. Last time Eva had looked a couple of chimps had been sitting there but now the branch was straining in the torrent and they were gone. She peered through the downpour and saw movement, several chimps climbing higher, others reaching down to help them. Something about their attitudes, the way they had gathered on the branches closest to the cliff, told her that they were in shelter – yes, of course, when she'd been out in the open with Sniff the wind had been from that side. Carefully she made her way across the network of branches and found she was right. It was like coming into a house out of the rain, so sudden was the difference. She went back and with some difficulty coaxed Lana to cross, and then Sweetiepie. Seeing them go, the rest came too.

There were barely enough perches to go round. Once they were settled Eva worked her way along the huddled line and counted. Eighteen, nineteen, twenty, twenty-one. All safe. But now she couldn't find anywhere to perch herself till Sniff shoved Herman over enough on the branch they were sharing to make room for her. She settled and looked at the torrent, trying to see if it was still rising. After that first tremendous buffet of water the downpour had lessened, though it was still heavier than any rain Eva had ever seen, lashed by the wind against the further cliff as if sprayed from firehoses. The whole mountainside must be streaming. If enough of it gathered here the ravine, as Maria had said, would fill right up, or far enough at least to tear the trees from their roothold in the cliffs. Before that happened they must move. The others, even Sniff, would be difficult to persuade, to make understand the danger. She set herself marks on the opposite cliff and tried to estimate whether the tumbling water was getting nearer. After a long while she decided it was, but slowly. No need to worry yet.

By then Eva had realized how cold it had got. At first her slight sense of chill seemed the natural result of drying out after her drenching, but even when she was dry she found she was shivering, and was glad of the warmth of Sniff's body. Not that it could have been cold by the standards of winter in the Reserve, but compared with the steady, steamy heat of the last week, when even chimps, who had evolved for a climate like that, had needed to rest through the middle of the day, the change was extraordinary.

How long did typhoons last? Two or three days, she seemed to remember. They were huge, intense .... sweeping along on curving .... get the

was going to g........................
of the tree they perched in were ....
They had already stripped the ravine of anything edible.

Time was impossible to estimate. The howling - minutes seemed like hours, but Eva noticed that as the wind rose the rain seemed to get less. Night would come with its usual rush, and then it would be pitch-dark, not even a firefly for guidance. Better go now. With a grunt of decision Eva started to move through the branches, then turned and made the 'Come' sign to Sniff. He looked at her as if she was mad but stayed where he was, and she went on alone.

There was no way out along the flooded floor, so she took the route Blossom had found up the further cliff. As she came out of shelter the wind seemed to lift her the last stretch and then try and blow her on up the slope above. Keeping low to the ground, clutching at bushes and boulders, she worked her way sideways along the slope and down into the valley.

Here the wind was less, no more than gale force, but above her it crashed through the straining tree-tops, making sharp explosions like gunfire where some big wet leaf was slapping itself to tatters, and shrieking between the thinner branches so loudly that Eva was forced to stop and stuff moss into her ears to try and dull the pain. The whole floor of the valley, including the patch under the palms where they usually slept, was flooded. She made her way round the edge of the water, down through the area of scrub and out into the open. The stream had gathered itself into a torrent again and was foaming down the mountain. The rain was almost over. She could see right down to the coast, and beyond that white foam and black water under a sky as dark as nightfall. Creeping close above the ground, clutching at boulders, she made her way to the place Dad had shown her, found the key and opened the steel chest. The chimp-chow came in five-kilo sacks. She took two out of the chest and re-locked it, then struggled back with one bag gripped between her teeth and the other under her arm. She had to leave the second one out above the ravine in order to climb down.

In the shelter of the cliff she worked along the line of chimps, distributing the chow by handfuls. They received it without any sign of surprise or gratitude and chewed away. They were calmer now, having realized that they were safer here than they would be anywhere else. Only Wang still kept his grin of terror.

Night came with just enough warning for Eva to move out and find herself a crotch to sleep in among the more exposed branches. With difficulty she persuaded Lana to do the same, and seeing what they were up to several of the others copied them. The rain came erratically now in rattling spasms, but a few drenchings were clearly better than dropping asleep and letting go of one's hold.

... ... cold, the snatched intervals

one had fallen. By now they took it ... Eva would bring them chow. Only Sniff was interested enough to follow her up the cliff for the second bag. The wind was wilder still, coming in heavy buffeting lumps. It was blowing half sideways along the slope now, so that Eva had to work her way directly across its path to where she'd left the bag pinned down by a rock. It was only a few metres, but she barely made it. Clearly there was no hope of getting down to the chest for more until the wind dropped. There was also no hope of persuading hungry chimps to let her preserve half a bag till the evening – in fact they were now confident enough of their safety to come crowding round when she brought the chow down, and have characteristic chimp-squabbles over their rations. Well, one evening without supper wouldn't kill them.

By late that morning the wind had gone round enough to blow directly up the ravine. For almost an hour it roared full-force between the cliffs, while the chimps clung with all their strength to the swaying branches, grinning their fright. At one point Eva remembered the cameras. Terrific pictures, she thought. Huh.

The wind swung on. They moved to the shelter of the further cliff and endured. Tomorrow, Eva thought. If it goes the same speed that it came. In the afternoon, when it's dying. Before the humans switch the alarm on again.

They spent the night hungry and cold. For several hours around dawn it rained, not quite as heavily as at the onset, but enough to wake the torrent below to another bout of white roaring.

As soon as the rain lessened Eva made the 'Come' signal to Sniff. This time he followed. Quite a lot of trees were down, including one of the shelter palms. She unlocked the chest, bit a bag open and let Sniff feed. She ate too. Then she gave him a fresh bag to carry and took one herself. At the top of the cliff she pinned one bag down and with some difficulty persuaded Sniff not to climb down into the ravine with the other, but to follow her on up to the top of the enclosure. The wind had picked their branch up and blown it against the fence – without that it would have gone right out to sea. They dragged it back, and, with Eva now helping her best and the wind behind them, dropped it without trouble across the top of the fence. Sniff watched frowning while Eva pinned the fork firm with several boulders, with the bag of chow beside it.

The branch bowed deeply when Sniff put his weight on it, but stayed in place and straightened as he walked four-footed to its stiffer end. He reached the top of the fence and paused, studying the drop. The wind screamed past, rumpling his pelt. Eva barked, anxiously. She'd known she'd have to take the risk of letting him get this far. Sniff glanced round.

up at the racing sky, turned, moved up the made the 'Come'

tion. Eva distribu

now, with everyone famished – and settled

ing of waiting. Most of it she spent grooming Lana, who paid little attention, being obsessed by Wang, inspecting every hair-root, turning him over and beginning again. Eva made occasional expeditions up the cliff, and now not only Sniff came with her. They moved around the wind-lashed slope above the ravine, nibbling the unappetizing leaves. The clouds were still low and dark, and moving very fast, and the chimps were nervous enough to go back to shelter almost at once.

Around noon Eva climbed out again. Sniff followed her as usual, and three or four of the others. This time she led the way down towards the palms. There were fallen branches all over the place, many with succulent young tips out of reach till now. Eva fed for a while, then broke off an handful of twigs and made the 'Come' sign to Sniff. He hesitated, grunted, and came with her, munching. At the ravine she climbed down and handed the food round, only a leaf or two each, enough to whet the chimps' appetites. They were hungry for greenery, and bored with being cooped in one place. Soon, in twos and threes, they were climbing the cliff and going to look for forage of their own.

Lana, preoccupied with Wang, was the slowest to move and Dinks stayed with her, but at length Eva managed to coax Dinks away, and Lana followed, rather than be left alone. With Wang clinging to her neck she climbed reluctantly up the greasy rock. Dinks had waited, and Sniff had been there all along, watching the process under frowning brows.

As soon as Lana came out into the open Eva snatched Wang from her back. He shrieked. Eva raced off, gripping Wang by his upper arm. Behind her she heard the racket of a chimp squabble, Lana's shrieks of outrage, joined by Dinks, and Sniff's hoot of warning. She paused and glanced round. Sniff was closest to her. He'd put himself between Eva and the other two and was following her up the slope keeping them at bay as he came. Dinks in any case was impeded by having Tod to carry. By climbing fast enough to prevent them from separating and one of them thus outflanking Sniff, Eva was able to lead the others on right up out into the open, over the ridge and down to the corner of the enclosure. Not giving herself a moment to hesitate she picked up the bag of chow, put it between her teeth and balanced herself out along the swaying branch. She gripped the projecting end with her free hand, swung herself down and dropped. She'd been worried that her weight coming down like that on the outer end would loose the fork from its mooring of boulders, but it didn't, and when she rose and looked round she saw that Lana must have been already on the branch, unintentionally weighting it firm.

Lana reached the top of the fence and balanced there, shrieking anger and fright and dismay. Eva ... her 'Come' sign and held Wang out, offering

Wang whimpered, his voice ... hiss of the wind. Lana overcame her doubts, swung on to the butt of the branch, dangled two-armed and dropped. The moment she touched the rocks she scampered to Wang and began inspecting him for signs of damage, turning her head every few seconds to snarl at Eva. On the other side of the fence Sniff was herding Dinks on to the branch. Twice she refused to go, huddling instead into the corner of the enclosure, but he cuffed her out into the open, rounded her up when she broke for the ridge and drove her back. The third time she did what he wanted – in fact once she was on the branch she barely hesitated, but seeing Lana below busy with Wang just dropped and joined her.

Sniff crossed last. His weight on the projecting butt of the branch, with no one to hold the inner end steady, dislodged it from the pile of boulders, and as he let go the spring of the fence tossed it back inside the enclosure.

While the two mothers calmed themselves by fussing over their babies, Sniff and Eva crouched side by side in the howling wind and studied the route ahead. The first part didn't look too difficult, a longish clamber across a slope of steeply tumbled boulders, but beyond that a rib of the mountain hid the next stretch and beyond that the angle became almost vertical, with the immensely steep slope of trees starting at the rim of a sheer cliff and rising into the cloud-base above.

Sniff turned his head and grunted to the others to follow. When they paid no attention he went round and chivvied them from the other side until they began, reluctantly, to move. As soon as he let them alone they sat down and returned to their babies. In the end it was Eva who had to find a route, while Sniff herded the other two along from behind.

By nightfall they were barely halfway there. In the dead ground beyond the mountain-rib they had found a sheer-sided cleft, like a great sword-cut into the mountain, only about thirty metres wide but impossible to cross. There were ledges here and there which they could have worked their way along, but none of them seemed to match with ledges on the opposite side. They explored for a crossing almost till dusk, and spent a bad night in a sheltered gully. They ate chow, and drank from a pool.

Eva woke next morning in a blaze of light. The storm had cleared the cloud-rack away and the sun was shining almost straight into their sleeping-place. The sea was rumpled still, but a dark clear blue under a paler, clearer sky. A lot of the plantation had been smashed flat. The moorings of the airboat seemed to have held, but one of the flivvers was on its side and the old factory by the harbour had lost most of its roof. Humans will be busy, Eva thought. Wonder how long till they miss us.

hours later, very faint

trees.

YEAR THREE, MONTH ONE, DAY FIVE

Living wild . . .
Hunted, in hiding, wary from dusk to dawn . . .
But living free.

Wang died on the mountain. It had happened on the first day of freedom. When Eva had left to explore their refuge with Sniff, Wang had been alive, huge-eyed, listless, panting, and Lana had huddled posses-sively over him, not letting anyone near. There had been the choice then to give up, for Eva to make her way somehow down the mountain, find Dad and Gerda, the expedition vet, get them back up (but how? Wind still too strong for the airboat, flivver use-less so close to this kind of slope) and by then Lana would be hiding, refusing help . . . It would never have worked, Eva kept telling herself afterwards. It was probably too late anyway – once small chimps started to go, even in the Pool, you usually lost them. Months, even years after, Eva would find herself pausing from what she was doing because the same old arguments had started running through her mind, with the same old guilt and sickness in her heart. By the time she and Sniff came back Wang was dead.

Lana had carried the body all next day, grooming and cradling and inspecting it at first, but by the third evening she was just trailing it around by a leg, like a child with a doll. Eva managed to keep herself awake that night. In the pitch dark, moving by feel, she stole the body away and buried it under some stones she had laid ready while she could still see. When Lana woke she was puzzled, and searched around in a vague way, but then let Eva groom her and be groomed in turn. Sometimes during the next few days she would seem to remember what she had lost, and start searching and calling, but in a few minutes she'd give up and go back to whatever she'd been doing

enclosure, perhaps because it was far
plantations and so there was less chance of crop-trees accidentally seeding up here and growing wild. Inside the wood you found that it wasn't one sheer slope, but a series of natural terraces that had trapped enough soil for the trees to get and keep their foothold, so the floor of the wood was like huge steps, a narrow strip of soil slanting up to a section of naked cliff, and then more soil before the next cliff. To move from strip to strip you climbed a tree. A lot of trees and branches were down after the typhoon, and in places the tangle was too dense for even chimps to find a way through. There were two streams, which joined near the bottom of the wood and fell over the final cliff in a narrow smoking fall.

Clinging to one of the last trees down there you could look out over the sea and the harbour and watch the flivver and the airboat rise and come and start looking for you.

On their first afternoon of exploration Eva and Sniff had seen a group of humans, tiny with distance, standing on the far side of the great cleft. From their attitudes they seemed more interested in the cleft itself than the wood. She guessed they were arguing whether the chimps could have crossed it. There were other patches of trees scattered across the rugged slopes of the mountains, any of which might hide the fugitives, and all of them desperately difficult to search in the damage after the typhoon. The humans would have to land a team from flivvers, somehow. It would be tricky, but they might manage it on the other side of this wood, where the step-like terraces ran out across the bare rock of the mountain face. Eva thought they wouldn't even try that until they found something to show that this was the wood the chimps were hiding in. The expedition hadn't brought any special hunting equipment with them, but they could send for it. What would they use? Heat sensors? Infra-red-detectors? Something like that, but it would take them a day or two to realize they weren't going to find the chimps without, and then several more days to get the stuff flown out. By then, if Grog was right, other things should have started happening . . .

You could hear the buzz of the flivver long before it came past, and freeze. Eva made a point of giving the warning bark whenever she heard it, deliberately sharing her nervousness with the others. She didn't want them getting used to it. The airboat was more of a problem because if the wind was right it could turn its engines off and drift along the mountainside in silence. Feeding chimps created a good deal of commotion in the tree-tops, bending and breaking branches to get at the tender leaves at the tips and generally crashing around. The typhoon had battered the trees enough for the damage the chimps did not to show, but in the hour or so before the evening rain, when the wind blew steadily from the north- out in that direction while she

for some while above the cliff beyond Objects dropped from the cabin at regular intervals. Eva could see the people up there in silhouette, holding things to their faces – binoculars? A shape changed, became familiar – a long-lensed camera. When the airship had gone and she went to see what had fallen she found the dark ledges flecked with coloured spots. Bananas, oranges. They would photograph them and check next pass how many had gone. If the whole lot vanished into the wood that would almost certainly mean chimps had got them. She did her best to warn Sniff with grunts and grimaces, and he got the message and refused to let any of the others out of the wood. They were all in any case by now infected with Eva's wariness of humans and other doings, and had enough to eat among the trees.

Next morning the airboat came back and checked. By then most of the fruit had gone, because a lot of burrowing marmots lived among the tree-roots and scavenged around at night. (Later Sniff taught himself a trick of lying in wait on a branch above the burrows and dropping on them as they emerged in the dusk. You gnawed the meat raw off the thin bones and didn't think about it with your human mind.) Several of the marmots lay around where the fruit had been, so some of the fruit must have been drugged. Eva guessed that Maria had the bit between her teeth again and wasn't listening to Dad. OK, he'd been wrong about leaving the chimps in the enclosure during the storm, but not for the reason anyone had thought of. He'd have known the chimps would carry the fruit away before they ate it, if Eva didn't manage to stop them. What use would a drugged chimp be, in among the trees? It would come round before anyone found it.

The fourth day, in the sticky stillness of noon when the wind was no more than a faint waft off the sea, the airboat came again. The whine of its motors stopped and it hovered in stillness over the tree-tops. An enormous voice broke the silence.

'Darling, please, please, for my sake, please come home . . .'

Unfair! Unfair on both of them. Eva stuffed her fingers in her ears. Poor Mum, she'd be pretty well frantic by now. She'd know Eva was due to come into oestrus in a few days' time – that had been one of the elements they'd had to consider in timing the whole expedition. Eva had already decided that when it happened she was going to let Sniff mate with her, if he wanted, which he presumably would. Why not? You couldn't choose some of this life, and not all of it. The airboat passed on. A couple of kilometres away it stopped and hovered again. She heard the voice very faintly, not the words, only the tone of pleading. Poor Mum. There must be another patch of trees over there, out of sight. That showed they still didn't know where the chimps were hiding.

came to the wood. They were

one over the trickier bits. Just before they r
trees this third man took off his helmet to mop his brow and Eva, watching from a branch three terraces further down, recognized him. He was Joey, the head keeper at the Reserve. He wasn't carrying a rock-axe but a stun-gun. He checked the mechanism before he went in under the trees.

When they struggled in along the terrace Eva followed them while Sniff led the others down to the lower end of the wood. She didn't dare get too close, so only caught odd glimpses of what they were up to. They didn't seem to be doing real hunting, but spent most of their time studying the ground, presumably for chimp-droppings and other traces, but they were out of luck. Because of the angle on which the trees grew, rising in tiers, rather more light reached the ground than it would have in a level patch of forest, and the going along the terraces was impeded by undergrowth, which also tended to hide the odd dropping that might have got scattered there. The hunters would have needed to chance on one of the places where the chimps nested or sheltered, and where the traces were much more obvious, but those were all further down the mountain. After about a couple of hours they called up the flivver on a commo, made their way into the open, and were hauled back up.

That same afternoon Eva noticed two small ships moored out to sea. They carried their own flivvers, which rose and started to scurry unsystematically around the mountain. Both flivvers were caught unawares by the evening downpour and must have had a tricky time getting back down. It didn't look as though they were part of the main expedition. There was plenty of room in the harbour, but the ships stayed out at sea, riding the slow ocean swell. A new airboat came past next day, loitering under the heavy sky, with a bright green bag and the letters ABS painted in vermilion along it. ABS was a shaper company, one of SMI's main rivals. Uh huh, thought Eva. Grog. Give us a month he'd said, if you can manage it. The way things were going she could have stayed out for years.

'You'll get world-wide interest,' he'd said. 'OK, you'll have that already, but it'll all be under SMI's control. They can turn it off like a tap if they want to. But you make yourself *news* in the middle of it and SMI can't copyright that. The rest will be round the island like vultures, watching every damn thing they're doing. If they put a foot wrong, the world's going to know. They'll be everybody's baddies.'

'They can sue us. They can make the Pool bankrupt.'

'They'll never dare. I think you could bust that contract anyway – I've taken advice – but it won't get that far. You've a very fair deal to offer them when they come round. Which they will. Just give me a month.'

came past, ... of noise because it was playing Tanya .... its loudspeakers. On the flank of its bag was the broken butterfly and a message: THE WORLD'S ON YOUR SIDE, EVA.

There were a dozen ships moored out at sea by now, and something passing overhead almost all day long. It became impossible to keep the chimps still while the watchers went by. It didn't have to be SMI who spotted them – any of the other companies would immediately send the pictures round the world, and then the rest would know. Eva realized that it had happened when she woke one morning and heard the noise, flivver-hum on twenty different notes and the deeper buzz of airboat engines. A big voice was calling from a speaker, and the Tanya Olaf music was blasting out, full volume. She couldn't hear any words above the other noises.

Climbing cautiously up through the tree where she'd nested, keeping close to the trunk so as not to sway the leaf-cover with her weight, Eva reached a point from which she could see several patches of sky. There was hardly a moment when one of them didn't have some kind of flying-machine passing through it. Something came rattling and tearing along the tree-tops to her left, and a moment later she saw the bulk of an airboat blocking out one whole patch. Under its cabin trailed a rope ladder. It wasn't the SMI boat. Perhaps they were hoping Eva would grab the ladder and scramble up and give them an exclusive interview. Crazy.

Soon there were people being lowered on to the bare terraces beyond the wood. Climbers with light ladders and ropes explored up and down for the least impeded routes into the trees, and then the hunting groups made their way in, parties of three, one carrying a gadget like a camera with a giant lens, as well as a stun-gun slung across his back, and one with an ordinary portable shaper with the SMI logo on its side. The first man pointed his gadget up among the tree-tops and also at any mound of fallen branches that looked as though it might be hiding something. Eva guessed it must be some kind of sensor which would register the radiation from an animal body, hidden among leaves. They worked systematically along the terrace while the flying-machines buzzed around overhead, invisible.

This was bad. She didn't know what to do. She had come to the edge of the wood to watch the landing, and Sniff had come too (he could smell that she was coming into oestrus, and wouldn't leave her side). The others were further down. There were at least two parties of hunters between them now. The chimps' whole instinct would be to climb for safety. They couldn't work out they were actually better off on the ground, provided they weren't on the same level as the hunters, because then the jut of the terraces would screen them from the sensor. Eva had trouble enough to get Sniff to stay down and wait for

move past, two terraces below.

a few met...

'They've located 'em. B Gang.

A passing flivver drowned any answers. By the time it had gone the men were picking their way back along the terrace. Eva and Sniff followed towards the edge of the wood and saw that one of the other gangs were out on the rock face already, waiting to be picked up by the flivver, ferried down the slope and landed again. The SMI airboat was hovering close in with cables dangling, ready to moor. In the sky overhead thirty or forty flying machines manoeuvred for a view of the hunt.

Sick in her heart, full of the sense of failure, Eva led the way down the terraces. Sniff came reluctantly, very nervous, constantly making small warning snorts and grunts. If he hadn't been so interested in her for other reasons he would probably have stayed behind. She took a route she knew well by now, mainly from tree to tree without touching the ground. She had no idea what she would do, could do. Hide by herself? Grog had said he could still have used her if she'd been the only one to get free. It wouldn't be easy. She'd need to hunt for food, to spend several hours on that. She had to sleep. And anyway Sniff would be tagging along. Bright though he was, he wouldn't understand about the sensors. Besides, alone wasn't enough. For Grog it might be, but Eva knew that a lone chimp is almost a kind of ghost, not quite real. It was the group that counted. From the very first she'd been determined to take Lana and the others with her. If they were caught, then it was all over.

Their route took them almost to the edge of the wood. The airboat was moored now, unloading what looked like nets. Yes of course. You couldn't just stun a chimp ten metres up a tree – you'd have to catch it as it fell, or it could be killed when it hit the ground. So if the chimps kept moving, if she could reach them and lead them away through the tree-tops . . .

It wouldn't work. They'd be terrified already, with the bustle in the wood and the racket of machines above. Their instinct would be to climb as high as they could, and cling. Without thinking what she was doing Eva continued on down until she was only a couple of terraces above the one on which the men were going to and fro. Here at last she paused and tried to think properly. Her mind buzzed. She felt as if she was being wrenched apart, back into her two selves, but it was her human mind which kept telling her that the best she could do was go and join the others and try and get them clear and if she couldn't then be caught with them, be shot and fall and fail – nobody would really get hurt if the hunters did their job properly. Her chimp half simply knew it had to hide.

Something happened while she was still hesitating. Through the buzz of engines she heard a new noise, a cry from throats, a human cheer. Instantly she under- someone had been caught. Too late. All

Eva waited. After some while the peop back, slowly, struggling to manoeuvre the stretcher over the difficult ground between the trees. They came and went, in glimpses. She craned. Somehow there always seemed to be an obstruction, a bush, a tree-trunk, the people themselves, between her and the pale canvas. Near the edge of the wood they paused. An argument began. Somebody spoke into a handset. Others peered out at the buzzing watchers in the sky above. A woman came scrambling across the rock from the airboat, carrying what looked like a sheet. Yes, of course. They didn't want the world to see them carrying a dead-looking chimp across the open surface between the wood and the airboat – bad image. The group parted to let the woman through, and now she could see the body on the stretcher. It was Lana.

Rage exploded. Eva didn't hear herself scream, wasn't aware of her rush through the branches till she saw the people turn and point, and a gun go up. The movement stopped her, changed the course of her attack. Even in the middle of the madness she knew she couldn't cope with people carrying stun-guns. If the man fired he missed. By then Eva was hurling herself out and down towards the edge of the wood, towards the open slope where the airboat was tethered. Perhaps some tiny part of her mind told her that if she could disable the airboat the people wouldn't be able to take Lana away, but all she felt was the need to attack, to break and smash and destroy. Anything human would do, and there was the airboat, huge and smug, trapped by its moorings on the rock below her. She picked up a loose rock and slung it. It bounced off the bag. Next time she aimed better and heard a crash from the cabin. The terrace on which she'd been hiding continued as a bare ledge across the rock-face, like the others above and below, before narrowing and becoming just part of the slope. Immediately above the airship it was blocked by a large boulder. Eva knuckled towards it, slinging loose stuff as she went. When she reached the boulder she gave it a heave, but it stayed firm. She started to scramble over it, looking for more missiles, but at this point she heard a grunt behind her, looked back and saw that Sniff had followed, and was bending to see if he could move it. She dropped on the far side, bent too and heaved. The boulder stirred. They grunted and heaved together, rolling it from its bed and over

226

the edge. It struck the rim of the ledge below and bounced, turning as it fell, straight into the cabin of the airboat, smashing clean through it and on in great leaps down the mountain.

Eva gave a great whoosh of satisfaction. As it ended something slapped into her arm, just below the elbow, hurting like fury. She looked down and saw the dart of a stun-gun protruding from her pelt. Before she could snatch it out she was in darkness.

Waking. Strange, drowsy, cold, the dream of trees . . .

moment there must be something . . . . eyes, but then she heard a grunt, and a face came close to hers, peering into her eyes. Sniff. Every hair of the grey whiskers below his mouth had a droplet of mist at the end. She grunted a welcome and eased herself on to her elbow to look around.

Of course. They were up in the cloud-layer. That was why it was so cold. They were on a ledge under a sort of fir with drooping branches from which dangled blobs of moss like seaweed, the shapes she'd seen in the mist. She knew the place. It was quite a long way up. The buzz of the flivvers and airboats came from below – less of them? Or just further away?

How long? What time was it? The drug from a dart usually lasted a couple of hours. She tried to sense where the weight of the sun fell, the way she used to when she lay in hospital . . . there. Early afternoon – that'd be about right. Plenty of daylight still for the people to find them. Straining her ears, filtering out the noise of the motors, she heard no sound of a hunt.

She felt decidedly sore. There was a cut in her thigh and bruises everywhere. Sniff must have carried or dragged her all this way, scrambling up from terrace to terrace, taking her with him any old how. Would he know about darts? Yes, probably. The keepers in the Reserve had to use them very occasionally, and if Sniff had seen it happen he'd have taken an interest, tried to work it out. Good old Sniff.

They stayed together all afternoon. No one came near them. When they looked for food they moved with caution. The trees were different up in the cloud-layer, with the fruit unripe, and little sweetness in the leaves. In the dusk, almost by accident, Sniff caught his first marmot. Just before it got dark they moved down to the warmer terraces below.

Eva woke hungry, but alert. No noises in the air at all – too early for humans. Cautiously she climbed a tree and peered around. The sky seemed empty, but there were a lot more ships offshore, three with air-boats tethered above them. The sky was its usual sullen layer, and the sea dark and slow-moving. Sniff joined her and looked around. They moved to a better tree and began to feed.

They were still there when they heard the motor, an airboat, not a flivver. They froze and waited. Over the wood the motor cut out and was replaced by a burst of music – the Tanya Olaf song. That stopped too. A voice boomed from a loudspeaker.

'Eva, this is Grog. Your Dad and I will be landing on the rock face to the south of the trees. No one else will be there. Can you come and talk?'

Starting and stopping its motor the airboat worked systematically up the hillside, repeating its message half a dozen times. When it came into view Eva saw it was the one with the broken butterfly and the message for her on its side. It could still be a trick, she thought. You couldn't be sure of recognizing Grog's voice, distorted like that, but she didn't care. She wanted to know what had happened to Lana.

Eva hooted, but they didn't hear the motors, so she lowered herself into the open and beckoned, then went back under the screening leaves and climbed on to a branch. Sniff watched from higher up, making little snorts of anxiety, as Dad led the way to the foot of the tree. He looked absolutely exhausted. Eva reached down and took her keyboard from him when he handed it to her. Immediately she tapped out a message.

'Sorry. I had to.'

'I'm aware that that is what you felt,' said Dad.

'Sorry.'

'Well, it's done now. I'm here in my legal capacity as your parent to tell you that I assent on my and your mother's behalf to the arrangement that Mr

Kennedy tells me you wish to make with your sponsoring companies, and which they in their turn have now agreed to.'

'Is Lana all right?' said Eva.

Dad blinked.

'She's fine, as far as I know,' he said. 'Haven't you seen her?'

'Uh?'

'They never took her off the hillside,' said Grog. 'They got a change of orders. I better explain. Your Dad's been having a bad time, and not just worrying about you. There've been some pretty severe personality clashes, with your Dad being accused of everything under the sun. On one side he can't help feeling you've let him down pretty badly, and on the other he's threatened with the big legal stick for helping you set this up. Right, sir?'

'Forget it,' said Dad. 'Tell her about the agreement.'

The bitterness in his voice wasn't quite real, Eva could tell. It was partly a kind of play-acting, putting himself in the centre of the zone and extracting as much drama as he could from the moment. What he really minded, probably, was Eva seeming to trust Grog more than she trusted him.

'It's really a sort of three-way, maybe four-way agreement if you count the chimps,' said Grog. 'World Fruit will set up a Trust with the Chimp Pool as joint Trustees. They lease St Hilaire to the Trust. They and SMI sponsor it. The Pool moves the major part of the Reserve out here. SMI to have exclusive filming rights, where possible by remote control cameras, and World Fruit exclusive commercial use of

230

any such film. Human access to be kept to a minimum – we haven't got all the detail worked out.'

Eva grunted. It was pretty well what Grog had outlined to her in Mimi's flat, several months ago, not what she really wanted, she'd felt back then, when the whole thing had seemed so nearly impossible that you might as well daydream it perfect, with no cameras, no sponsors, nothing to do with the human world. Now it was going to come true she realized it was better than she could have hoped for. It was amazing.

world Fruit Boardroom, said Grog.

while – I'd heard rumours, of course – I've got a couple of contacts. None of them's interested in chimps, as such, but what they do care like hell about is their image. This Maria woman is a protégé of a fellow who's part of a faction . . . hell, it's too complicated to explain, but what you've got to think of is the board members sitting round watching the pictures coming in from St Hilaire, and on another couple of screens getting the figures for world reaction to what they were seeing. Not too bad at first. Nothing to look at but trees and rock and flivvers nipping around. Lot of interest, though – they'd *loved* the stuff from down in the other wood. They'd got pretty well the whole world watching, waiting, wanting to see what was going to happen. And what did they see? Look, I've brought some stills . . .'

Grog took the pictures out of a case and passed them up. Eva leafed through . . . They'd been taken from above, at an angle, and all showed the same scene, the bare rock ledges, the bulge of the airboat's bag, its shadow heavy on the rock, the edge of the wood at the side. At the top of the first picture, black and tiny like spiders, two chimpanzees were knuckling out along a ledge. In the next the leading chimp was throwing something. Then they were both heaving at a boulder. Then they were looking down the slope, side by side. The boulder was gone and the bag hid what had happened to the cabin of the airboat, but the attitudes of the chimps spoke like a language – you could see their sense of achievement, their aggression and resistance, their sense of their own wildness and freedom. In the next picture one of the chimps was sprawled on the ledge and the other was bending over her, while in the bottom corner – the viewpoint had shifted slightly – one man was trying to raise the barrel of a stun-gun while another was trying to force it down. The next picture showed Sniff carrying Eva back along the ledge. He had somehow got her across his shoulder and was knuckling along three-footed, gripping her left arm with his right hand. The last picture was a close-up of the same thing. It too spoke. Looked at with human eyes, thought about with a human mind, felt with human emotions, it almost cried aloud. All the old stories were there, the sort of thing people saw in cartoons and adventures on the shaper practically every day of their lives, the lone fighters against impossible odds,

232

the rescue from the battlefield under fire, the comradeship in the face of death. Uh uh, thought Eva. People. They'll never understand. Not why he did it at all.

'Chap who shot you had lost his head,' said Dad. 'If you'd fallen off that ledge you might have been killed.'

'That's only part of it,' said Grog. 'One of my contacts told me that when those pictures came through, and the world reaction on the screens, the people at World Fruit as good as panicked. Some of them had

herself up to where Sniff was pull....

screening leaves. If she'd been able to open her mouth she would have whooped as she went. He peered, frowning, at the pictures, turned them over and studied their blank backs. She knew he could feel her excitement and happiness, but he couldn't understand the cause. She wasn't even sure that he could read the pictures enough to understand that the small black blobs were chimps, let alone realize that one of them was him. The human meanings, the stories of defiance and comradeship, would mean nothing to him at all. All he wanted was to move away with Eva through the tree-paths, back into the depths of the wood, together. Eva gave him a chimp-kiss, then detached herself and swung back down.

'That Sniff?' said Grog. 'Won't he come and shake hands?'

'Uh uh.'

Dad was looking at her with an inquisitive gleam in his eye. He would have seen her rump as she'd climbed. Eva gazed blankly back. It was nothing to do with him, nothing to do with any human. Her feelings for Sniff and Sniff's for her were not even like human ideas about sex and love. You mustn't try and bring those ideas in. You must let it happen as it would have happened in the forest of the dream, with the human Eva no more than a guest at the wedding, accepting and approving. Eva reached for the keyboard.

'You can tell Mum I'm OK,' she said.

Dad looked disappointed, but shrugged. Bound to happen one day, he thought. He'd want to set up a research project, of course, as soon as a baby was born. He wasn't thinking of Eva as his daughter any more, any more than he would think of that baby as his grandchild – which it wouldn't be.

'Can you face a press conference?' said Grog. 'Sooner we can get a commitment in public, the harder it'll be for the bastards to cry off.'

'Uh.'

'Ok. I'll set it up for this evening. Down by the harbour would be easiest – there'll be a fair amount of equipment to fly in.'

'No. Here. Under the trees.'

PART THREE
DYING

YEAR TWENTY-FOUR, MONTH FORGOTTEN, DAY FORGOTTEN

Dying . . .
Sun high, warm on the pelt, but chill inside . . .
Yellow-grey mist, vague shapes, buzzing . . .

years before, recovering from her last illness,
got Dad's *Diseases of the Chimpanzee* out of the storage box and read about strokes. It had been difficult even then, with her right eye misty with cataract and her left too short-sighted to make more than a blur of the letters. She had managed it with the magnifying glass, but she couldn't have done now. Anyway there was no point. She was dying.

The others knew. That was why Hruffa had stayed with her to meet the humans – she'd never done so before. Hruffa was shivering with nerves, and was grooming for her own reassurance as much as Eva's comfort. Eva raised her good hand and began to search along Hruffa's shoulder, with her muzzle pressed close in an effort to see among the hair-roots.

She found a tick by touch, cracked it between her nails and ate it.

The motor of an airboat drubbed from beyond the trees. Hruffa twitched with anxiety, and Eva pursed her lips and made the little sucking noises chimp-mothers use to calm a frightened baby – noises she'd used when Hruffa herself had been a springy pink-and-black scrap clutching her side. The buzz became louder. She could sense all the others, in among the shadows under the trees, watching. They too under-stood it was the last time.

Eva nodded to herself. She stopped grooming Hruffa and moved the hand to the keyboard where it hung in its loops on her chest. Extraordinary how her fingers still knew the letters which her mind seemed almost to have forgotten. Slowly she pressed a few keys.

'Hi there. Just testing.'

Hruffa jerked at the human voice. Eva reacted more slowly but more deeply. Over the past twenty years she must have got the keyboard out and used it dozens of times, hardly thinking about it at all, con-cerned only with what was to be said, not the voice that said it. Now, this last time, she was ambushed. The pang of ancient loss, a child with long black hair ice-skating in a yellow tracksuit. Me, whispered the ghost, the real Eva.

It was part of dying, coming in two like that. Hruffa must have felt the ambush, because she put her long arm round Eva and hugged her, rocking both bodies gently to and fro.

The airboat motor cut. It must be in sight by now, huge in the blue winter sky, but Eva couldn't see it.

Higher-pitched, a flivver detached itself, hummed down, settled in a storm of gusted leaves on the other side of the clearing. Through her misted vision Eva saw the people take shape, two moving tree-trunks tramping towards her over the dusty earth. By their movements and sizes a man and a woman.

'Hello, Eva,' said the man.

'Denny?' she said. She had recognized the voice and was surprised. Denny was Director of the whole Chimpanzee Pool, but he'd taken on being Director of the Trust as well when Grog Kennedy's mental ill-

treatment, but she'd refused, just as she'd always refused any help of any kind after the setting-up stage. If the chimps couldn't do something for themselves it didn't belong on the island.

'Right first time,' he said. 'I'd like you to meet Gudrun Alp, Eva.'

Eva gave a grunt of welcome and held up her hand. She could sense the tingle of excitement with which the woman took it – she'd never touched a chimp before, so she wasn't anything to do with the Pool.

'Hruffa,' she said, and then because to human ears the name would sound like a meaningless bark she spelt it out on the keyboard.

'Hruffa, my daughter.'

Hruffa held out her hand, unprompted, and the people took it.

'Pleased to meet you,' they said.

Few of the humans who'd visited over the years had really come to terms with the idea of Eva having children. Chimp kids. In their minds there were images of white women being carried away into the jungle by giant apes. They were both uneasy and inquisitive. Once when someone had asked about her newest baby who the father was Eva had laughed and said she didn't know. There'd been a silence, a change of subject. Eva could have told them chimp societies don't work like that, with a woman and a man falling in love and setting up house. You could be fond of a particular male, excited even by him, but your affection was for your group, and your love, if you were a female, was for your own mother and daughter. Eva hadn't bothered to explain because that was not what the meetings were for. In her eyes their only purpose had been to get the project set up and after that to see that the humans stayed happy with things as they were, and didn't come to the island except for the meetings. When people asked the sort of question people did ask, out of the endless human longing to know, she answered as briefly as possible.

'Your mother sent some grapes,' said Denny.

'And her love,' said the woman. Eva nudged Hruffa to take the grapes. Hruffa started a grab but remembered that this was a moment of ritual. She took the bunch and tore off a twiglet which she put into Eva's hand. Eva ate the grapes slowly, bursting them one by one against her palate. Last time, that shock of sweetness.

240

While she ate the woman came and squatted on her other side. People sometimes did that, trying to conduct themselves chimp-fashion, but with them it had usually been a deliberate decision. This woman, Eva sensed, had done it naturally, without thinking.

'I'm afraid Lil's not too well,' she said.

Eva grunted understanding. She held out her hand for another twiglet of grapes and when Hruffa gave it to her she passed it on to the woman, who took it and ate.

lot of kids have been taking their own lives. No reason anyone can give. I lost my own daughter five years back. Lil helped with our counselling group. I cracked up more than some, but Lil was pretty good to me and in the end we kind of elected each other mother and daughter. We had good times, considering. She never talked about you outside the counselling group, except these last couple of months when she's been getting old tapes out and playing them through and through. Then she asked if I could make it out here, see you. The Trust laid it on. They said you've not been too well yourself. I haven't told Lil.'

Eva grunted.

'D'you think I should?' said the woman.

'You decide. Say I understand. Thank you for coming, Gudrun. And for loving Mum.'

Silence again. Eva rested. It had been an effort to press so many keys, to order her thoughts into a human mode.

'Trees are coming along nicely,' said Denny.

It was just conversation, but he sounded as if he was trying to cheer himself up by talking about something that had gone right. And it was true. Eva was proud of the trees. She'd planted most of them herself, in the gaps of the old plantation, using seed the Trust had gathered and sent, food trees and shade trees. Most of them had failed, or been smashed by a passing chimp in a temper, but enough had come through. Trees grew fast in this climate. More important still, there were saplings growing which Hruffa had planted, and Whahhu, and some of the others. Not all of them, but a few, because they had watched Eva doing it when they were small. It was something you did. Eva treasured the day when Hawa had taken her to show her a stem that had burst from the ground overnight, splaying its cotyledon leaves apart. Hawa must have planted that seed herself, and remembered doing so, and had made the connection. Yes the trees were worth it, and so was everything else.

Denny coughed.

'I've got some other news,' he said. 'It's pretty important. Do you feel up to it?'

'Uh.'

Eva felt very clear-headed, very aware. Though she couldn't see as far as the trees her perceptions seemed to reach out all round her. She could feel the invisible watchers in the shadows, waiting.

242

'Fact is, they're closing down the Pool. Winding up the Trust, too.'

'Uh?'

Eva wasn't surprised. The past half-dozen visits she'd sensed some kind of change in the air. And the technicians not coming to service the cameras – things like that.

'We've run out of funds,' said Denny. 'It isn't just us. There's hardly a project that hasn't got trouble. It's the same all over. You can't get a bridge built, or a solar replaced. You can't get a road repaired. People

...y daughter joined a group which walked into the sea,' said Gudrun. 'They put rocks in their pockets, joined hands and walked in, singing. Just a couple of dozen kids. Now they're doing it hundreds at a time. When Lil goes, I think I might try that.'

Denny didn't protest. He took it as just one of the things people said and did these days.

'So it's no more of these trips, Eva,' he said. 'I don't know what it'll mean for the chimps.'

Eva moved her hand carefully across the keyboard.

'Will they leave us alone?' said the young voice.

'No telling. No telling about anything. We've not been here before. Sometimes I think it's just a phase, old Dame Nature who we keep forgetting we're children of just cutting the population back to a sane kind of size, and then we'll start again. Sometimes I think it's not a long step from walking into the sea with rocks in your pockets to deciding to blow the whole planet apart, clean sweep. I don't think that's going to happen. It'd take more organization than we'll be capable of much longer. I suppose there might be a war or two. Won't last. Nobody's got the will. No, funny thing is that the people who bother me most are the ones who'd try and tell you they're on your side. There's been a lot of potty little sects sprung up, and we've had a bit of trouble in the Trust from a group who call themselves Kennedyites, after old Grog. Their idea is that chimps are the human future. They call you the Inheritors. It's all mixed up with eleven-dimensional super-intelligences in hyper-space but there's always a chance some of them might trek out here and beg you to come back and save the world.'

'Ask them to keep away.'

'They don't pay any attention to me. Apparently I'm an emanation of Antitruth. I suppose you could try sending them a message by Gudrun . . .'

'I don't imagine anyone would listen to me,' said Gudrun.

Eva bowed her head, collecting her ideas. She would like to send a message, she thought. It didn't really matter who to. One by one she chose the keys, concentrating, using the last little driblets of human energy. At last she pressed the 'Speak' key.

'Hello,' said the unchanged voice. 'This is Eva. I am speaking for all the chimps in the Reserve. I want to say thank you to the humans for giving us back our proper life. We are well and happy. We will be all

244

right if we are left alone. I don't know what is going to happen in the rest of the world, but if the chimps survive it will be because of what you have done for us. Thank you.'

She took the keyboard from its loops and pressed the key to eject the tape, but instead of taking it out she pushed the cover shut and handed the whole keyboard to Denny. She heard the click of the cover opening and made a rejecting movement with her good arm.

'Uh uh,' she said.

Eva could hear the defeat in his voice, the defeat of humankind and all that cleverness, all those machines they'd used to control the universe, lost in the silence of a tape which had nothing to play it. She hunched her shoulders to the sun. She was going sooner than she'd thought. She hoped she wouldn't die before she got back under the trees.

The people rose.

'I'll give your message to Lil,' said Gudrun. 'And your love.'

'Well, goodbye, Eva,' said Denny. 'It's been a privilege to have known you. Goodbye, Hruffa.'

They shook hands and moved away, became tramping pillars, columns of mist, nothing. The flivver hummed and the downdraught buffeted across the dry earth. The noises dwindled into the sky.

Now Eva's own group came out of the trees, carrying the litter Whahhu and Graa had made. Eva's third daughter, Hawa, brought a half-gourd of water. Eva drank a little and let Hawa bathe her face while Hruffa handed round the rest of the grapes. There was a spat between Graa and Arrwa about the share-out but almost before Hruffa and Whahhu had barked at them they remembered where they were, and why. Eva let herself be lifted on to the litter and carried back towards the trees.

The others came out to meet them. She could feel their solemnity. They knew. Of course they had not asked themselves if the humans would stop coming once Eva was no longer there to talk for them. There was no way Eva could explain something like that, not even to Hruffa. All she could do was let them understand that a change was coming – not by telling them, but by feeling the approaching change inside herself, by sharing the feeling, and her own acceptance of it. They joined the process, sharing and understanding. They knew.

There would be other changes which Eva herself had long foreseen but which there was no way of sharing. The structure of the groups would alter – they would become more separate without Eva's prestige to bind them. The dominance of the males would become more marked, and would shift slightly in other ways. Eva had always understood that she had to work within the grain of nature, her own and the others'. It had been no use, for instance, supporting Sniff indefinitely once Abel had grown into a big

246

strong male, and almost as intelligent. Poor Sniff had
become very morose and withdrawn, but it couldn't
be helped. On the other hand she herself had always
refused to mate with males she thought stupid or
unsociable, and sometimes by guile and distraction
had interfered in the same kind of way when the
other females were in season. That wouldn't happen
any more.

The names, she thought, would probably go too,
though not long ago Hawa had brought her new
baby to her and told her his name, unprompted.

advantage for chimps with vocal tracts slightly more
adapted to naming to be the ones who had more children . . . hard to see how.

Fire-making, though. Knots. Making and using a
bone needle so that leathery palm-leaves could be
sown into a shelter and your baby stay dry from summer downpours . . . The litter on which Eva lay was
of special importance to her. It wasn't the first – Eva
had made that, years ago, to carry Beth from place to
place when her legs became paralysed. Later she'd
shown the others how, and supervised. Their main
use was for carrying food, and things like bedding
materials, up into the caves. This one had been made
by Whahhu and Graa. Eva herself had taught

Whahhu, and Whahhu had taught Graa. Graa, more-
over, was a male. Eva had found him when he was
still only half grown, high up in the mountains on a
clear winter day, staring at the distant blue loom of
Madagascar. Graa was Sniff's grandson. If you could
make a litter, perhaps one day you would experiment
with a raft.

No. It was far too soon. Generations beyond generations would have to pass before that, or before
you could say that the skills had become enough of an
advantage to be passed down in the genes, slightly
nimbler fingers to make the knots, slightly subtler
minds to think of uses for them, let alone for the new
race of chimps to begin to move outward. Quite likely it would never happen at all – quite likely people
would change their minds and come back and wipe
out the chimps – but if it did those far distant adven-
turers would not be Eva's descendants. They would
be Hruffa's, and Graa's, and Arrwa's, and Urff's – and
Kelly's. Not one human gene would be there. Only,
faintly, but in all of them, changed by them and
changing them, the threads of human knowledge.

Our gift to the future, thought Eva. It crossed her
mind to wonder what had happened to Dad. Denny
hadn't said anything about Dad.

At the edge of the trees but still in the sunlight her
bearers put the litter on the ground and stood back.
Eva lay on her side in the useless warmth. If they'd
propped her up she would have fallen. All she could
see was a dark band between the glare of the sky and
the glare of the bleached earth, but she could feel the
presence of the others, hear their breathing and their
mutters of doubt and concern. One by one, in no

order, they came forward and crouched in front of her, panting lightly, putting their faces close enough for her to smell their breath and see the glint in the dark brown eyes. They reached out and touched her thigh or forearm, or the back of her hand. The ~~~ ers helped their children to perform th~~~ ritual. The ones with small b~~~ moment against her si~~~

When they b~~~

Their ~~~

~~~ ~~~ ~~~ ~~~ aught ~~~ ~~~ in it and pile ~~~ now on, their voices ~~~ ew. They would have to con- ~~~ er, and survive.

~~~ ie end they left her alone to die. All of them, even Hruffa. She could not see them but felt them go, splitting into their groups and families and then, like something happening in a dream, moving slowly away into the trees.

PETER DICKINSON

AK

leads the guerrilla group, and his mother is the war.

Peace comes – and Paul buries his gun and goes to school. But it does not last. Soldiers come to burn the school and kill the children, and Paul must flee through the bush to find his gun and then . . .

Will it be war once more, or is there another way?

A selected list of titles available from Macmillan and Pan Books

The prices shown below are correct at the time of going to press. However, Macmillan Publishers reserve the right to show new retail prices on covers which may differ from those previously advertised.

PETER DICKINSON

The Kin: Noli's Story	0 330 37311 0	£3.99
The Kin	0 330 39225 5	£6.99
The Lion Tamer's Daughter	0 330 37164 9	£4.99
Eva	0 330 48384 6	£5.99
AK	0 330 48204 1	£4.99
The Ropemaker	0 330 39713 3	£6.99
Tales of the Salamander	1 403 02051 2	£9.99

All Macmillan titles can be ordered from our website, www.panmacmillan.com or from your local bookshop and are also available by post from:

Bookpost
PO Box 29, Douglas, Isle of Man IM99 1BQ

Credit cards accepted. For details:
Telephone: 01624 836000
Fax: 01624 670923
E-mail: bookshop@enterprise.net
www.bookpost.co.uk

Free postage and packing in the UK.